THE HERON RIDE

On a warm, summer evening, at
sundown, Sandra and her brother Adam
stood in a cottage garden, watching a
line of riders cantering across the
skyline of the Downs. Sandra – for
whom life had been tough and sad –
longed to be riding with them. But
for her there was no horse, and there
was no money.
This is the story of how she and Adam
became so involved in the fortunes of
these six riders that, in the end,
her luck turned

The Heron Ride

Mary Treadgold

Illustrations by Victor G. Ambrus

KNIGHT BOOKS

ISBN 0 340 02426 7
This edition published February 1967 by Knight Books,
the Paperback Division of Brockhampton Press Ltd,
Salisbury Road, Leicester
Fourth impression 1974

Printed and bound in Great Britain by
Cox & Wyman Ltd, London, Reading and Fakenham

First published in Great Britain
by Jonathan Cape Limited 1962
Text copyright © 1962 Mary Treadgold

With love to EMILY ANDERSON

I

'I'm never going to look right on a horse . . .'

Sandra – twelve years old, small, thin, pale, and dark-haired – clutched at the snaffle, ducked, and fell silent as Toby moved in under the cluster of beech trees. The summer leaves brushed across the top of her head. The cows, drowsing in the long grass by the stream, moved off, startled. A pair of dragon-flies swept in to the shadows to meet her, and swept out again. Adam, naked to the waist, down in the shallows with his rod, drew back the over-hanging trailing branches to peer up at her, before calmly turning back to the sun-splashed water.

Once in the shade of the beech trees, maddening Toby subsided, standing still and solid like a great fat bulrush, listening apparently to sounds beyond meadow, hill and woods that he alone could hear.

'No fish.' Adam had tactfully ignored his sister's cry. 'Not a bite. That otter from that Mill Pool's been around again,' he added smoulderingly, as he played out more line. Down in the stream, bent nearly double squinting at his float, at thirteen he looked even smaller than Sandra, skinnier and more wiry.

Up under the beeches Sandra relaxed into the old borrowed saddle. The sun had come chasing after her into the cavern of green leaves, flecking her scalp and pricking her arms. It was too warm to be *agonized*. But it could still be *disappointing*. Nobody could ever, ever look right upon fat Toby! She slid her feet out of the hot stirrups, so that her legs dangled down Toby's portly, hairy flanks. Toby continued to stand motionless, his Roman nose thrust forward, as if the mere notion of any shift of stance were repellent. Nobody, thought Sandra, would have guessed that three minutes ago Toby had been ungraciously heaving himself round Long Meadow – jogging and stopping until he had nearly pitched off his far-from-expert rider by plunging malevolently into the teeming August hedge to take a fancy sniff at some cow-parsley. . . .

She looked down at the back of Toby's ears. He must have known she was looking because they began to twitch. She started to laugh. Oh, but he was funny – a pompous pony. Really, he wasn't unlike Uncle Arthur – only nicer . . . It was wonderful to be with a horse who was nicer than Uncle Arthur. Giving his tousled mane a friendly little pat, 'It's not really your fault that you're so fat,' she told him gently, 'I ought never to have expected you could go like a Derby winner, and if you had, I'd have fallen off.

I don't ride well enough. I ought to have guessed that an odd-job pony wouldn't be a riding pony when Miss Vaughan said the Vicar had offered to lend you . . .'

'Can't hear,' said Adam, without turning.

'Well,' began Sandra more loudly, 'well, the fact is I simply haven't had enough lessons, even if he weren't so fat. And I hated having to ask Uncle Arthur for any at all. Only I did so very much want to learn. So I asked him in the middle of Piccadilly Circus one Sunday afternoon. The cousins and Aunt Lucia had gone on ahead. That was during last term when you were away at school. But next morning I heard him chewing his scrubby little moustache – you know, how he does when he doesn't like spending money – and then he said to Aunt Lucia that he didn't want me to get what he called "horse-minded", in case I got as keen as Mother was . . .'

'Why ever shouldn't you get as keen as Mother was? She wasn't *silly* about horses, was she ?'

Adam's gaze was still devotedly fixed upon his little red float, idling out in the deeper, greener, darker waters beyond the trees. 'I remember Father saying – what was it ? – that she was a magnificent horsewoman. That must have been when we were in Vienna – or was it Budapest ? I don't remember. Anyway, Uncle Arthur ought to be jolly pleased if somebody in the family were within a throw of Mother – and not only because of her riding. But I suppose he'd be jealous, because,' finished Adam dispassionately, 'he's a mean-minded little man.'

Sandra checked a twitch from Toby, as a fly penetrated the shadows and played insolently round his thick nose.

'As a matter of fact, I heard him say he didn't want me to get ideas, because I wasn't going to have an easy life like Mother when I was grown up.'

'I don't know why he should have thought Mother's

life was all that easy. Being a diplomat's wife isn't. It may
be *different* from being a solicitor's wife – Aunt Lucia
couldn't be a diplomat's wife if she tried.'

'Well, anyway, in the end, and because of all that, they
turned out to be pretty scruffy riding-lessons,' said Sandra
pacifically. 'He unearthed a riding school out beyond Put-
ney – the kind that aims at getting your money quickly –
you know, gone-at-the-knees horses, and the woman who
taught got up in wonderful jodhpurs, but rotten at the
job. . . .'

Sandra's voice trailed away at the recollection, and for
some minutes the only sound in Long Meadow was a lark
singing high up over the Downs beyond the trees, now
hidden in the heat-haze. It was difficult to be suitably
grateful to Uncle Arthur for that handful of hopelessly
inadequate lessons in the London suburban riding school,
run on the cheap, with its miserable bony hacks, heads
down, dispiritedly hip-hopping along the side of a tarmac
by-pass.

A threatening little gulp came up Sandra's throat before
she could stop it. She knew this little gulp. It was an old
enemy. She told herself in panic: I mustn't think about
it all. I mustn't think about those *other* horses. I mustn't
remember what it was all like *before*. . . .'

Before they had come to live with Uncle Arthur! It was
too late. She had thought, and she had remembered. And
what with the disappointment about Toby, and the flood
of memories, quite suddenly the little gulp came right up
into her mouth and the tears began to cascade down her
face. For the very breadth and peace of the countryside
had itself been quietly reminding Sandra during the past
five days of that other life before Uncle Arthur – that
heavenly other life with Father and Mother, where she
could just remember horses very different from Toby and

the poor old by-pass hacks – beautiful, elegant horses that had stepped proudly along as if they loved the world.

'I must say . . .'

The silence was broken by the voice of her brother down in the stream, and the sound of him reeling in his line. Because of the tears she could see at least six little scarlet floats streaking for the bank. Luckily Adam was apparently too absorbed to turn round. 'I must say,' he went on, 'I was deeply thankful when I got your letter at school to say we were being sent down to Sussex instead of going off for another ghastly holiday with the cousins in another sea-side town like last year. I didn't care who Miss Vaughan was, or what Long Meadow Cottage was like. I merely folded your letter, and stuffed it into my locker – and I said – I said . . .'

'What did you say ?'

'I said, "Well, thank goodness, we shall have a month away from our kind guardians and our lovely home in Beastly Bayswater. Perhaps at Miss Vaughan's – whoever she is – there'll be some *peace*, and we can get on with things." '

Sandra let out a long, shaky breath. She knew just what Adam meant. She knew that what he and she both wanted was to be left alone to get on with their lives together – after the long, dreadful separations of term-time. They wanted peace to be somewhere together that was not that hateful, over-crowded London house, packed with yelling, quarrelling cousins, which was all the home that she and Adam had known for the past four years – the bad, black years since Father and Mother had both been killed in the car-smash high up on the cold Brünig Pass in Switzerland.

'It's different here from Uncle Arthur's,' she said tenta-tively to the absorbed figure down in the shallows. And then she added, 'Even though it's quite a small cottage –

somehow it's all more like – what it used to be. It reminds
me . . .' and she broke off. Since Adam had been sent to
boarding-school, and she had seen so little of him, she was
never quite certain whether he still cared to be reminded
of that other life with Father and Mother. He never seemed
to want to talk now of the distant cities where they had
once lived, or of the different houses that had once been
home. He would make the occasional glancing reference –
as he had just now – but that was all.

Sandra sat very still in the saddle. They had both come
a long way from the Beautiful Cities, as Sandra called
them to herself. Berne – Vienna – Budapest – the cities
where Father had held his various appointments – they
were now only places on a map in a geography lesson, or,
if she ever spoke their names over privately to herself, like
a kind of music she had once heard. And the houses too.
Sandra stared down at Adam, now disentangling hook and
float, with the shadows from the beech leaves speckling
his back. Did he remember – also with aching homesick-
ness – the houses they had lived in? The square white
house with the overgrown garden and the purple bougain-
villaea flowing down the walls? The tall grey house in the
silent street with stone swags of flowers above each
window?

'*You'll none of you see a more wonderful house than
this!*'

Sandra remembered – and she wondered if Adam remembered, too – Father crying it out, like a fanfare, every
time he helped haul the luggage over yet another wonderful threshold, in yet another Beautiful City, even more
splendid and exciting than the last. And did Adam remember
that, in every house, there had always been Father and
Mother in and out of the nursery, always there, and
always, so it seemed for ever afterwards –

'Laughing. That's what I most remember about them.
They seemed always to be laughing,' Sandra had once
said yearningly to Adam, after they had been taken to
live in Uncle Arthur's house in London, where nobody
was gay, but only noisy, and the laughter was either
giggling, or never happened at all. . . .

Sandra was still dreaming in the saddle – seeing the
houses and the cities, hearing the lost voices – when she
heard Adam say, 'There aren't any fish. And it must be
nearly tea-time.'

He had disentangled everything, packed up his rod and
line, and was clambering up the bank towards her. She
watched him struggle into his shirt. The nearest cow
moved off with an alarmed swish of the tail, as his arms
flailed the heavy summer air. Then he stood straight up,
and looked directly at Sandra.

'It's worse for you than for me,' he said sombrely.
'You're there – with them – the whole year round.'

But Sandra was already feeling that she should not have
spoken. In her heart she knew that it had been hard on
Uncle Arthur and Aunt Lucia to have two silent, unhappy
people, so different from their own children, suddenly
added to the household.

'They mean to be kind,' she said. 'And it isn't just that
I'm being hateful. It's not just that I don't like sharing a
room with Sue, and having Peter and Oliver teasing and
criticizing. It's – it's –'

Adam had jammed his linen sun-hat on his head. With
fishing gear in hand, he came over to stand at Toby's near-
side.

'What is it, then?' he asked, his thin, goblin face looking much older than its years.

Sandra struggled to keep back further tears, to find the
right words.

'We've been there for four years,' she burst out at last. 'And we're still strangers. I still don't fit. I don't feel I belong. Adam, I don't seem to belong anywhere – to anybody. . . .'

The little distressed cry, going up so solitary there in the meadow under the empty blue sky, seemed to disturb Toby. He sawed his head up and down, and then began of his own accord to move slowly forward, plodding laboriously out of the green shelter, out into the sunlight of the meadow.

Adam walked alongside. His head was bent, as if he were searching for something lost in the dried, colourless grass of Long Meadow. Then he looked up at his sister, who was riding along as if she would die before she shed another tear.

'It won't go on for ever,' Adam said slowly and distinctly, for he had learned in his life that bad things do pass. 'Some day we'll be grown up, and they'll have finished educating us, and then we can say thank-you, and leave Uncle Arthur. We can go and have a house of our own, and we can earn our own money to pay for it.'

Sandra tried to smile at him, to be hopeful, too.

'In the meantime, we've got a whole month here,' he went on. 'And you did say you liked it, didn't you? You did say you liked staying with Miss Vaughan?'

At his last anxious words, a small watery smile straggled properly across Sandra's tearful face. 'Oh, I do,' she said. 'I didn't expect to from what Aunt Lucia said about her. I didn't see how one could like being with a really old-fashioned retired governess, and I didn't think anything nice was ever going to happen again. But it has – and oh yes, I *love* being here.'

They walked along in silence for some minutes. Then unexpectedly Adam began to laugh. After a second Sandra made an effort, and joined in – alternately dabbing at the tear-stains and making a clutch at the reins.

'You don't know what I'm laughing at,' cackled Adam, falling over the landing-net in his paroxysms. 'You haven't a clue. It's *you*. You riding! Why do you suddenly want to? It's so unlike you. You never used to be the sort of girl who wanted to bounce round with a Pony Club in one of those little black velvet caps and a yellow pullover. You must have wanted it jolly hard to tackle Uncle Arthur about lessons, seeing how scared of him you are.'

Here Adam lurched up against Toby – who blew offend-
edly at him – and said 'Sorry' to Toby, not Sandra.

Sandra sat as upright as she could manage, and gazed
ahead at the landscape with a suddenly remote dignity.
Her recent recovery from tears was too precarious to risk
telling Adam why she wanted so much – so very much –
to ride. Some time, of course, she would tell him. But not
now.

She was saved by Adam all at once stopping dead.
'Hello,' he said, pointing. 'Look what's coming. Talk of
Pony Clubs –'

'It's not. I know what it is. Oh, I wish they didn't have
to see me looking so awful on Toby. It's not a Pony
Club . . .'

They stared, open-mouthed, at the far corner of the
meadow, where, beyond the hedge, a cavalcade of heads
came bobbing along the lane, nearly hidden in a cloud of
white dust.

'They go up to the Downs every day about this time.
It's the Riding Holiday School – out beyond the village.
It's called Greens because some people called Green owned
it,' said Sandra, seizing the opportunity to slide off Toby,
so that she could look as if she were just about to mount
him. 'Miss Vaughan told me all about it. I'd love to go
there, but it costs money. The Greens have just sold it to
some man who's very well known in the riding world. And
it's going to become famous like his other school in the
West of England. He's going to build it up.'

'But who goes there ?'

'Well – people like us, who haven't anywhere to go for
the holidays. They get taken for riding picnics all over the
Downs, and this new man's going to teach jumping.'

'*Not that lot taught jumping – goodness, just look at
them!*'

The cavalcade was now in full view, coming up to the five-barred gate between Long Meadow and the lane up to the Downs – four horses topped by four riders, passing at an ambling trot.

'That's never going to be a famous riding school, my girl! My goodness, there's not one of them can even ride! You look better on Toby. Jumping my foot! Look – three girls, one boy. Don't they all look bored! Hey, that little brown one like a gipsy, with the gilt ear-rings – she'll be off in a minute!'

'Sssh. Adam. Stop. You're shouting.'

But Adam could not stop. He had been upset by Sandra's upset. The steam was now escaping.

'Well – look at them. That girl with the pony-tail. Hello, one's turned round.'

The last rider – a little girl of about ten, with a round, smug face, and a carefully combed mop of honey-rinsed

hair, turned a bright, apprehensive glance in the direction
of the staring Sandra and Adam, before vanishing.

'She must have heard, Adam. You're bellowing.'

'I'm not bellowing. She ought to be on a leading-rein.
And I've seen that child somewhere before. I know that
winning smile. Oh, I say – that must be the new owner.
Golly!'

Past the gate, bringing up the rear at some distance, riding smoothly, nonchalantly, as if he lived on the dark bay,
went a heavy, oldish man in a blue riding-shirt. He had a
lean, sallow face with a small grey moustache. As he
passed, he turned his head in the direction of Adam, glow-
ering furiously. Then he, too, was gone.

'Well!' said Adam eloquently in the middle of Long
Meadow. 'That was a bad-tempered individual, if you like.
I don't care what anybody says about him being well
known. Did you *see* his face! Why, it was – it was *yellow*
with bad temper. He looked like the Demon King in that
pantomime we saw at Christmas! And *did* he hear me!'

II

As the sound of the trotting hooves died away up the lane
curving towards the Downs, Sandra said, faintly alarmed:
'It's not his fault his face is like that.'

'Yes, it is,' said Adam, glaring in his turn at the gateway
across which the Demon King had ridden. 'People's faces
are like them. Look at Uncle Arthur's face – that's got just
like him – pinched and mean and bullying. People's faces
become – what's the word I want ? – *transmogrified!*'

'His name's Mogg,' said Sandra.

'*Well!*' said Adam, awed to momentary wordlessness by this fascinating coincidence. 'How on earth did you know that?'

'It was when Miss Vaughan was telling me about Greens. She said it had been taken over quite unexpectedly this summer by this Major Mogg.'

'He looked about as fed up as they did. Perhaps Greens doesn't want to be made into a crack riding school.'

'I should think that's about it,' said Sandra. 'Miss Vaughan said it had always been a very small, homely sort of place, where nobody bothered much about riding well, but all the children absolutely loved it.'

But Adam's attention was already engaged elsewhere.

'Whoa there! *Toby!* You let that pony bully you like Uncle Arthur. Why don't you stand up to him?'

Bored by the attention devoted to other people's horses, Toby had spied the clump of oaks in the Glebe, the field beyond Long Meadow that hid his Vicarage. He was walking determinedly off, the reins gently tugged out of Sandra's preoccupied hands.

Sandra gave a little shriek, and stumbled off in pursuit. The tea-time sun blinding his eyes, Adam watched her lead Toby over to the Glebe gate. Then, pushing his sun-hat back on his head, he stumped slowly up towards Miss Vaughan's cottage, where it stood at the top of Long Meadow, white and low and peaceful, against a background of apple trees. His pointed face was concentrated and angry, and he stubbed at the cropped grass with the butt of his landing-net.

'Drat him,' he muttered. 'Drat him. Drat him.'

And it was not Major Mogg, the Demon King, whom he dratted, but Uncle Arthur – because he also could remember those other days when Sandra, like his mother and father, had always seemed to be laughing. He recol-

lected her as he had seen her only a week ago, on the first
day of the holidays, sitting quietly among the cousins
round the long Bayswater supper-table. Now he came to
think of it, she had seemed to be smaller, and paler, and
thinner than when they had been together at Easter. She
had looked somehow – quenched. Staring down at the
Long Meadow turf, Adam made a colossal effort with his
imagination – she had looked like a girl who had been
out in the snow and the winter cold for a long, long
time. . . .

Sandra had, meanwhile, turned Toby loose in the Glebe,

and was carrying the borrowed saddle and bridle back to
the garden-shed at Long Meadow Cottage. She also was
walking slowly. But she was not thinking about Uncle
Arthur. She was thinking about Greens – and Adam. Her
mouth turned up into a smile at his awful behaviour. She
knew that he was quite unaware of it. Then a small sigh
escaped her. The Greens' horses had looked pretty good
horses. They were a lot better than Toby – better, too, than
those poor old bags-of-bones she had ridden in London!
But – Sandra paused at the white gate leading from the
meadow into Miss Vaughan's garden – Greens' horses
were not so fine as those she had once seen with Mother.
Absent-mindedly Sandra pushed the gate open. Slowly she
crossed the grass to the shed. What *were* those horses
that she could never quite remember ? Where *had* she seen
horses so splendid that ever since no horse had seemed
quite splendid enough ? It had been years ago – when
she was quite small – and Mother had taken her ...
Mother had taken her ...

Sandra deposited the saddle and bridle in the corner of
the dark garden-shed, and came out again into the sunlight. Where *had* Mother taken her? It was no good. The
elusive memory of those wonderful horses had escaped
her again. Had it been – at a circus – in Berne? Or Budapest ? She seemed to remember them *indoors*. No – it was
no good. And it didn't really matter. But those *had* been
horses! And those were what, in her heart, she would
like to ride – even if she couldn't yet manage to stay on
Toby! She'd like, at any rate – she decided, as she walked
up the little path between the snapdragon beds – to see
horses like that again. Perhaps – if she saved up, and paid
for herself – Uncle Arthur might be persuaded to let her go
next year, just once, to Olympia. . . .

At this point Sandra became aware that she was just

coming up to the small Queen Anne door into the cottage, and that a peculiar silence overhung the place. Through the open door she could see Adam's linen hat cast down on the settle in the hall. But not only was there an absence of voices – worse, there was an absence of tea-time noises. Those cheerful noises that five days of Long Meadow Cottage had encouraged Sandra to associate with tea – old thin china clinking, silver spoons clattering, and copper kettle singing. She crossed the little, square, white-panelled hall into the drawing-room, and there –

'What did I see?' she declaimed five minutes later to Adam and Miss Vaughan.

'You saw, confronting you, Miss Mogg, the Demon Queen – as like the Demon King as two peas – and you gave a yelp,' said Adam coldly, 'and then you saw Miss Vaughan and me, standing like a pair of corpses, with our jaws dropped, because I'd just—'

'Most unfortunate,' said Miss Vaughan.

'Because I'd just come charging in – I'd been cleaning up for tea in the cloaks – and saying –'

'At the top of your voice,' said Miss Vaughan.

'*That we'd seen a perfectly ghastly-looking old boy, herding a riding school that couldn't ride up the lane*. Well, how could I know that it was his sister calling on you, when she was standing half behind the door and the sun was in my eyes?'

'It was lucky that Sandra arrived just then,' said Miss Vaughan placidly. She had seated herself in the window-seat to fold up her square of embroidery – a little elderly lady, elegant as her tiny drawing-room, upright as a small knitting-needle, with a twist of iron-grey hair on top of her head.

'We shouldn't, my dears, judge people entirely by their appearances, but I am bound to admit that when the front door bell rang, and I saw Miss Mogg standing on the doorstep –'

'All oily. She looked terribly oily. Rubbing her hands round each other as if she were washing –'

'– I was not impressed –'

'*Impressed!* You should see King Mogg,' burst in Adam again, dancing from one foot to the other. 'Gosh, aren't they unlucky to look like that if they want to make money with their riding school! D'you know what I think? I think they're both *murderers!*' he finished morbidly.

'Adam.' Miss Vaughan calmly laid the coloured strands of embroidery silk side by side on top of the folded square, and rose to her feet. 'I've not yet met Major Mogg, but he has been in the past an internationally distinguished horseman.'

'Well, I only marvel his horses haven't jibbed when they've turned and looked at his face. You just *wait!*'

'Perhaps you'll bring in the tea for us,' Miss Vaughan said firmly, and led the way down the two dark polished steps at the end of the drawing-room into the minute octagonal dining-room, that had hollyhocks bobbing against the window-pane, and a view down Long Meadow up to the Downs.

'As a matter of fact,' conceded Miss Vaughan from the head of the tea-table, 'I was not at all sorry to be able with perfect truth to refuse Miss Mogg's request.'

'You don't mean to say –' Adam had re-entered the room with the teapot – 'that she had the cheek to want something?'

'Miss Mogg made a perfectly reasonable request. She'd heard in the village that since my retirement I occasionally receive children as paying guests for the holidays.' Taking no notice of his yearning glance at the chocolate cake, Miss Vaughan had received the teapot, and passed Adam a plate of plain bread-and-butter. 'Apparently the Moggs' present house – Greens – is quite full up. It's a very small house – far too small for the expansion Major Mogg had planned.'

'Oh, *silly* man! *Why* take on something . . . too small!'

'Well, not entirely silly, Adam. They took over the last few months of the lease, because the Greens wanted a quick sale, and Major Mogg wanted to take over a going concern, and not to have to start it up afresh. Now, it seems, they have another pupil arriving, and there has been something of a muddle over rooms.'

'Did she want to off-load on to *us*? I *say*! Dash it! What a nerve!'

'Not at all, Adam. The new large house that her brother has bought for the venture is not yet ready. It's perfectly natural that there should be problems of this kind arising when there has been a transfer of proprietorship. Miss Mogg had simply encouraged herself to hope that I might be able to accommodate the boy here for them at short notice.'

'Another boy'll be a jolly good thing, I should think, from what Sandra and I saw of them all just now. All those girls! There was a fat sulky one with her hair in a straggly pony-tail who looked as if she needed a man's hand. I didn't think much of *her*. And I know I've seen the smug child with the ever-so-sweet hair somewhere.'

'Probably on television,' said Miss Vaughan. 'Miss Mogg was telling me that they had a child television star learning to ride for her career.'

'That's it. That's it. She's Ethne Blake. Child-heroine-saves-baby-brother-with-aid-of-horse. I knew I'd seen her. Ugh! *Terrible!*'

But Adam's attention was already on the wane, because Miss Vaughan had plunged the cake knife into the chocolate cake. His mouth began to curve into a slow, pleased,

anticipatory smile. Miss Vaughan glanced at him, and
eased a large slice on to his plate. She smiled back at him.

'Oh,' said Sandra to herself. 'I do like her.'

Who could ever have thought that Aunt Lucia would
have been so right about Miss Vaughan? 'Why, she's a mar-
vellous person!' Aunt Lucia had boomed, after the two
children had been told that they were to be sent to Miss
Vaughan. 'She's the real old-fashioned English governess –
been abroad teaching in private families all her life. There
are very few left like Miss Vaughan now. You and Adam'll
love her.'

And so, astoundingly enough, it had proved. Half an
hour after their nervous arrival at Long Meadow Cottage,
Sandra was chattering away more expansively than at any
other time during the past four years, and Adam already
seeking Miss Vaughan's expert advice about his favourite –
and, to many, peculiar – hobby of taking brass-rubbings
in local churches. It was all very, very surprising. . . .

She came to to hear Adam saying complacently:

'Well, we've got, haven't we, the absolutely cast-iron
excuse for not putting up Queen Mogg's extra boy? I mean,
us. That was what you meant, wasn't it? You really
couldn't fit anyone else in, could you?'

'No?' said Miss Vaughan, her head a trifle on one side.
'No? Well, now, I wonder . . .'

Adam, who had been swinging his chair back, suddenly
righted it with a small thud.

'Oh,' he said, eyes ostentatiously rounding with assumed
horror. 'Could I guess what you're thinking of? *The Little
Refugee Child!* I'd forgotten – but completely forgotten.
Oh, how could I!'

'I don't know, since we have discussed his arrival in-
cessantly,' returned Miss Vaughan blandly. 'And why,
precisely, do you refer to him as "little"? From the inform-

ation sent to me by the refugee authorities in whose charge
he has been, he appears to be some few months older than
you.'

'That's what that refugee appeal said – the one that kept
arriving through the letter-box for Uncle Arthur,' said
Sandra. 'It was always asking for money, and saying,
"Won't you take a Little Refugee Child into your heart?"
Adam said the refugees he remembered in Vienna were
fierce and angry and tough, and wouldn't feel like being
grateful enough to Uncle Arthur, even if he did take one,
on top of us, into his stony heart.'

'I am not necessarily taking Paul into my heart,' said
Miss Vaughan, 'not unless I like him, that is. I'm merely
offering him a month's holiday in this country. But, yes,
Adam – it was certainly Paul I was using as an excuse to
Miss Mogg.'

Adam had been considering his plate. Now he raised his
eyes seraphically to Miss Vaughan.

'I know it's very good of you to have invited a Little
Refugee Child from Europe's Ravaged Lands, and I do
know you'd invited him long before Uncle Arthur wrote
to you about Us,' he said in the winsome tones of a mar-
tyred child-saint. 'But do we have to have him, do you
think? Won't it rather spoil things – somehow? Seeing it's
all being so nice, and you and we get on so well together?'

It was lamentably clear that, upon behalf of himself
and Sandra, Adam considered Long Meadow Cottage a
pretty good berth. It was a pity to be called in the name
of suffering humanity to share it.

Miss Vaughan eyed him without a word. Sandra thought
that they were like actors staging a duel with mock swords –
each enjoying the other's performance.

'I can just remember the refugees in Vienna,' she said
softly – almost to herself, for she did not think Miss

Vaughan and Adam were really listening. 'When I was a
very little girl. They weren't all tough. I remember some of
them – all huddled together in that big open place – outside that huge church –'

'The Stefanskirche –' said Miss Vaughan.

'It was cold.' Sandra frowned, her face sad and lost in
recollection of that winter's day. 'There were men and
women – they looked so frightened, and there were some
who were crying, and babies, and other people with arm-
bands and food, trying to comfort them. They'd come, my
nurse said, a long, long way . . .'

'All the way from Hungary. And they didn't belong anywhere any more. I remember them, too,' said Miss
Vaughan. 'I also was in Vienna then. That's when I made
up my mind – when I saw them looking so lost and so cold –
that some day, when I had bought my cottage, I would
invite a refugee to come for a little while to England.'

There was a silence in the dining-room. Then Adam said
suddenly, 'Sandra's rather like that kind of refugee, isn't
she ?'

Sandra jumped. But Adam's eyes were fixed anxiously
upon Miss Vaughan. The play-acting was over.

'Yes,' said Miss Vaughan gently to Adam.

Sandra looked from one to the other. 'I'm not a refugee,'
she said, puzzled. 'Why –' and then, without warning,
happiness unexpectedly surged up inside her, the kind of
happiness born of sun and the country and loving people
that she had forgotten, because it was so long since she
had felt it. 'Why, I'm – I'm *here*,' she proclaimed triumphantly, pushing back her chair and jumping to her feet with
the surprise and the excitement of being happy.

They washed up the tea-things in the kitchen, Miss
Vaughan doing the washing, and Sandra and Adam the
drying. While they had been eating their tea and talking,

the torrid August afternoon had been quietly giving place
to early evening. When the china had been put away in
the corner cupboard, the three of them went out and stood
between the two tall cypresses, pointed like birthday
candles, upon the lawn. It was cooler, but the air was still
warm and sweet with the scent of flowers. In the garden
the mallows were just beginning to fold limply, the apple
leaves in the orchard to be a darker green as the longer
shadows crept among them. Down Long Meadow the cows
had left the stream, and were slowly munching their way
towards the middle of the field.

Sandra gave a little cry. 'Look –' and pointed up to the
Downs, from which the heat-haze had lifted. 'They've got
there,' she said.

There they went – the line of riders that the children
had seen earlier in the lane, strung out now in formation
along the clear, rolling ridge of downland. High up there
in the evening sun, nobody's horse looked anything but
wonderful, and nobody's riding looked bad. All of them
seemed like those other fine horses and riders that Sandra

remembered, as if in a dream, from her former life. She stood, lost in happiness, watching them canter away over the close-cropped turf, until the last horse and rider had disappeared over the ridge.

Then – 'Look – look – up there,' shouted Adam suddenly. 'There's something on fire over there – look, it's blazing!'

Sandra followed his excited pointing arm. 'It's a house,' she cried, 'someone's house is on fire!'

They raced across the lawn to the white fence, and hung over it, straining, with their hands cupping their eyes, to see more clearly across the valley, where, on the way up to the Downs, stood a large grey house, half hidden in trees, that they had never noticed before. Now, like a great ship, it was blazing from end to end with lights of golden fire.

Miss Vaughan came up behind, and put a hand on each shoulder. The children turned to her. She was smiling. 'It's the sun catching the windows,' she said. 'It does that every evening at this time. That's the house the Moggs have bought for their big new riding school. It's called The Heron. It's a *beautiful* house.'

III

A COUPLE of days later, before breakfast, the children went down to the stream to find the Mill Pool, with a view to tracking the marauding otter.

So early in the morning the stream, down by the trees, was smooth and impenetrable as dark glass. They followed it past the spinney beyond Long Meadow, after which it crossed two more fields, and plunged quickly into woods so tall and dense and silent that the children's voices died away in awe. Half in, half out of the water, toes curling into mud, they scrambled noiselessly along, clutching on to the ivied roots of trees, until they came at last to a divide in the stream, tossed a coin, took a chance, and followed the left-hand fork, which curved into an arched green tunnel of trunks and undergrowth. Just when Sandra was about to whisper 'We're lost,' the current began to run more swiftly, weeds began to stream along the surface like banners, and, on the far side of some overhanging oaks, the stream widened farther, farther until it turned a corner and became a large pool, its water suddenly golden-brown and cheerful, because the sun was now high enough to fleck it through a gap in the trees overhead.

'Now that's odd,' said Adam, clinging perilously to a gnarled trunk, and staring up beyond the derelict clap-board mill rotting at the far end of the pool. 'See where we've got to?'

'There's a lane,' said Sandra in surprise, tilting back her head and following his gaze up the steeply mounting woods, and then: 'It's that house of King Mogg's we saw the other night. We must be right at the very bottom of the valley. All the way the stream's been winding slowly towards The Heron –'

'– while the lane from Long Meadow to the Downs goes winding slowly up through the woods and past it. They must pass The Heron every evening on their ride up. What a gorgeous position it's going to be for a riding school! Far better than stuck away outside the village like Greens.' Adam sat down interestedly at the edge of the pool.

Framed by the mossy tree-trunks, splashed by the sun-light, the Demon King's demesne, hidden in the woods, looked just like a fairy-tale kingdom. Old and asleep, en-closed by a high wall covered with moss and lichen, the grey, dreaming house ensnared both children with its en-chantment, so that for some minutes they sat side by side, dangling their feet and gently swishing them to and fro through the clear water, thinking their own thoughts, and staring up at the long line of empty windows. Then simultaneously they sighed, got up, and, doubling over, began to search the edges of the pool for signs of the otter.

There were no signs. After a little while, they forgot the otter, were lured by the pool, slipped off their clothes, and slid down into the cold waters, swimming idly and floating on their backs, blinking up at the sun, now rising high through the tree-tops.

'Sssh.'

Sandra raised her head, and stared up at the house.

'Adam –'

Adam swam noiselessly towards her, his questioning face glistening with water.

'There's somebody up there,' whispered Sandra. 'Listen – there it is again.'

They slid, like water-rats, beneath a huge empty arc of tree-roots, reaching up out of the water to hang on to the dried branches, floating their limbs, and peering up at The Heron.

They could see the large, blank, double-fronted gates in the high wall shake, as they were opened from inside, and then . . .

'He can't see us, can he ?' breathed Sandra, terrified.

Adam shook his head. They watched, fascinated, as King Mogg stepped through his gates, turned and locked them after himself, and hid the key behind one of the loose stones in the wall. Then he stood, dusting his hands down his breeches as if he had not a care in the world, and finally strode off down the lane, disappearing from view. A minute later, the children heard a car start up.

When the noise had finally died away down the hill, Sandra said shakily.

'I can't think why I'm so scared of him. After all, we don't really believe he's bad. All he's done is to glare at you over a gate when – if you don't mind my saying so – you'd asked for it. And he's not here as a burglar. It's his own house.'

T—B

'Since you feel he's so cosy, would you fancy going up and having a look inside The Heron?' said Adam. 'I bet I could find that spare key of his in the wall.'

He shot off backwards in a flurry of spray across the pool, and then trod water, mopping and mowing wickedly at Sandra.

'I'd rather go home to breakfast,' said Sandra.

They pulled themselves wet into their clothes and set off, drying as they went, under the sun, which was now properly breaking into the woods, streaking the tree-trunks and setting all the leaves twinkling.

'Why is it called The Heron?'

Sandra broke a long silence, as they clambered over a fallen tree-trunk, lying almost across the stream.

'Because years and years ago, a heron flew up from the marshes and liked the garden. It used to come and stand there on one leg on the lawn. They could see it from the windows at daybreak. It looked quite at home always, and so the people called the house The Heron, as a kind of compliment to that heron.'

Adam skipped briskly over hooping trails and tangles of bramble.

'How did you find that out?'

'Miss Vaughan told me. She'd been in to see the garden before King Mogg bought it. It's quite wild, and she says there's a little old lead heron standing in the middle of a pond somewhere.'

'They must have been nice people who put it there for that heron's sake.'

'She says she hopes King Mogg leaves the garden alone, because it's beautiful as it is.' Adam turned to pull Sandra up the bank from the stream, where she had found an easier path than among the undergrowth.

As they finally turned up Long Meadow, with the stream

at their backs, Sandra said, 'We never seem to be coming up this meadow but what we're in search of food.'

'Hoo,' said her brother trustingly, '*she* doesn't mind. *She* knows we need feeding up. *She* knows people like us are always hungry.' Inconsequently, he ended: 'Her name's Eulalia.'

'How ever do you know that ?'

Into this inane conversation-piece, the next event in the curious sequence of the following week then broke.

There was a sudden, high-pitched shrieking, as if a small bat lurked around Long Meadow Cottage, which was apparently still wrapped in sleep like The Heron. Then, round the corner of the cottage, at break-neck speed, hurtled two figures – a tall figure in pursuit of a tiny one. Standing transfixed down the meadow, Adam and Sandra saw the tiny one, still emitting the little shrieks, slap open the white gate, and come running, running blindly until, with an extra piercing shriek of shock, it cannoned straight into Sandra's outstretched arms as she neatly stepped across its path.

'There –' said Sandra tenderly, bending over the small, shaking object with a sheltering gesture.

'*He were on tiptoe, he were, at the larder window. Standing on a flower-pot. I seen him.*'

The taller figure, who, by his uniform, seemed to be the local telegraph boy, drew up by the little group, scarlet and panting and bellowing as if everybody required ear-trumpets.

At the same time, Adam's Eulalia could be seen hastily making her way from the kitchen end of the cottage.

'*Had his hand right through the window. Little thief!*' bawled the telegraph boy up the meadow to Miss Vaughan.

As the little boy burrowed his ginger head further into her jeans, Sandra gently uncurled one clenched hand.

There, for Miss Vaughan to see as she joined them, lay a triangle of cake, the icing now neatly transferred on to Sandra's palm.

'I had to leave m'bike, and this isn't m'job . . .'

As if by the airiest sleight of hand, from out of the bluest of summer morning skies, Miss Vaughan produced some money, and the telegraph boy bounced himself off – and,

to Sandra and Adam's pleasure, had sheepishly to return
to hand over his telegram.

When he had finally departed, for a little while nobody
said anything. Down by the stream bird-song rose joyfully from the trees. Beyond the valley a train could be
heard distantly chugging out of earshot. Otherwise there
seemed to be no sound in the whole world. Miss Vaughan,
Sandra, Adam – they all stood patiently waiting in the
middle of the meadow.

At length – still dramatically wailing, though with dimi-
nishing intensity – the ginger head was cautiously raised.
From beneath the lank ginger thatch, green eyes slewed
vigilantly from Sandra to Adam, from Adam to Miss
Vaughan. In turn, they stared down at the small face –
lean, pearly-white, freckle-dusted – and terribly, terribly
familiar.

'I can't take it.' Fanning himself, Adam staggered about
the meadow in assumed faintness. 'King Mogg. Queen
Mogg. And now Baby Mogg.'

'I'm *not* Baby Mogg, even if I do have to live with
Moggses. I'm *Willy* Mogg – and the other children call me
Weary Willy, cos I cries a lot, an' if you tell me great-
auntie or me grandfather about the cake, they'll *be-eat*
me. . . .' And down Weary Willy's woebegone cheeks,
as from the overflow pipe up at the cottage, poured the
tears.

Sandra's mouth was already down-turning in sympathy.
But Adam and Miss Vaughan, maintaining flinty counten-
ances, fixed Weary from either side with the gimlet eyes of
accusation. Cautiously glancing from face to face, Weary
rightly came down in favour of Sandra, and slid his hand
hurriedly back into hers.

'I wuz going for me after-breakfast walk,' he wept, his
mouth widening in a crescent of self-pity. And then, as he

recollected another grievance: 'All the others have horses to go. There isn't *any* horse for me!'

'And do you so much want to take your morning walk on a horse?' inquired Miss Vaughan crisply.

'N-no,' said Weary, startled into honesty at the horror of the idea, and moving hurriedly to his next grievance. 'Me great-auntie, she was turning me out of me little bedroom, and putting me to sleep on the kitchen *flo-or*,' he proclaimed, gazing round the circle to assess his effect.

This time it was Adam's turn. That gentleman was standing no more, and wanted his breakfast. 'You know, I bet it's a jolly comfortable floor,' he said heartlessly, planting a finger between Weary's shoulders, and beginning to propel him up the meadow towards the cottage. 'I bet you've got a good cosy shake-down, and if it weren't for this hot weather, I bet it'd be right up against the stove.'

'Ye-es,' reluctantly agreed Weary, his short legs beginning to rotate faster and faster as Adam remorselessly steered him towards the white gate.

'And what about our cake? Yes – that bit of nastiness flat out on my sister's hand?'

Seizing the opportunity to slow the pace: 'I wuz hungry – *starvin*',' announced Weary melodramatically, his voice thickening with sobs at his own pathos. 'An' I saw the little winder . . .'

'Now never mind the window, little boy.' Miss Vaughan, who had dropped behind to open her telegram, came briskly up on the other side of Weary. 'What actually did you have for your breakfast?'

'Sausage,' said Weary.

'*Well!*' said Adam, hands on hips, glaring down at Weary. 'You lucky little devil!'

'It was only half a sausage,' said Weary. 'An' it was such a *very little* sausage to start with.'

He looked anxiously from one to the other again. And, curiously, on the small face this time was the look of truth.

'I think,' said Miss Vaughan, taking the situation quickly in hand by shepherding a slightly ashamed Adam and Sandra through the white gate after Weary, 'I think that, in that case, you had better go home by way of my kitchen, because Sandra and Adam and I are just going to cook our own breakfasts – and perhaps we can find a *very little* rasher of bacon to keep the sausage company. . . .'

'It's the oddest thing how we keep running up against Greens,' said Adam, when Weary had been sped, trotting down the road – beaming, greasy-mouthed, and trustful. He and Sandra and Miss Vaughan were clustered again round the kitchen stove. 'First of all, we see pupils who'd disgrace any school, riding past Long Meadow, looking like a lot of death's-heads. Then we meet Queen Mogg oiling up to you. Then we spot a house which turns out to be King Mogg's new premises –'

'Then we get a close-up of King Mogg himself on the new premises,' put in Sandra. 'Oh, I forgot – we haven't had a chance to tell you yet –' and she threw an affectionate arm round Miss Vaughan, while she prodded the bacon in the frying-pan with the spatula in her spare hand.

'And now, last of all,' said Adam, 'Baby Mogg.'

'I liked Weary,' said Sandra happily. 'I loved him.'

'Don't flick me with bacon grease.'

'I didn't!'

'You did!'

'I liked Weary, too,' said Miss Vaughan, diplomatically grasping the coffee-pot, and leading the way into the garden.

When Adam had set the breakfast-tray down on the long wooden table on the grass, the trio drew in their chairs under the shade of the apple trees. Ahead of them,

down Long Meadow, the cows were already making their
way, with swinging rumps, towards the stream to begin
another summer day's idling. Dangling his stick, the
leisurely boy who had shepherded them across the Glebe
was already plodding back towards the gate. Already the
heat-haze was starting to blot out the Downs, so that they
seemed like only the giant shadows of clouds against an
invisible horizon.

But, from the woods that clothed the slopes of the
Downs, The Heron was still standing out in relief. Holding
out her cup for coffee, Sandra thought that the lane Greens
took every evening up to The Heron – and far beyond –
must be a wonderful ride. Past Long Meadow, over the
stream it would go – and then wind up, up through the
tall woods, until suddenly it would come on the old mossy
wall, and the great gates, and the high chimneys of The
Heron itself.

'Oh, even if they are all bad riders, so am I. And I'd love
to go up The Heron Ride with them,' she said longingly
to herself. And then she remembered something else.
'And I'd love to dismount at the gates, and go inside, and
find the little lead heron hidden in the garden,' she added.

'Now I come to think of it,' Miss Vaughan was saying, 'I
do remember his great-aunt – whom you are calling Queen
Mogg – telling me that they had had to give over a bedroom to her brother's small grandson. The little boy's
father – Major Mogg's son – has apparently deserted the
mother. And she cannot cope with Weary for the present,
so the Moggs have had to take charge of him. I gather he
will be there for some time.'

'Like us with Uncle Arthur,' commented Sandra, for-
getting The Heron, and tilting back her chair to gaze
blithely up into the green depths of the apple trees.

'Uncle Arthur, at any rate, doesn't give us only half a

very little sausage for our breakfasts,' said Adam. 'Do you suppose Queen Mogg is economizing on all the house-keeping? Because that would account for them all looking so miserable a couple of evenings ago.'

'Actually I feel rather distressed about little Weary,' said Miss Vaughan. 'I do not, in point of fact, imagine that his grandfather and his great-aunt do ill-treat him. But, from my observation of him this morning, I don't think that he has a very happy life with them.'

'Well, he said his great-auntie and his grandfather would *be-eat* him.' Adam gave a passable imitation of Weary. 'And they've already turned him out of his bedroom. Still, he was a pretty awful little phoney, wasn't he? I mean – most of that performance in the meadow just now was an act, wasn't it?'

'Weary is what the French call *un original*,' observed Miss Vaughan in an impeccable French accent. 'That is to say, he is like nobody but himself –'

She broke off, because Sandra had given a little jump.

'I remember Mother using that word.' Sandra was look-ing at Miss Vaughan with a sudden delighted smile of recognition. 'It was years ago, and we were in a garden then, too. Only it was quite a different garden. It was the one in Vienna, and it was all overgrown, and there were big purple hanging flowers – and I was on a garden-seat, and Mother was telling Father that Adam was an *original*.'

'*Me?*' Adam paused in mid-swipe at a wasp dawdling its August way through his marmalade. 'Me? An original?' As Sandra and Miss Vaughan looked gravely at him, a slow, pleased smirk stole across his face. 'Hmm,' he said, attempting to keep his gratification from appearing too obvious. Then – detachedly – 'Oh, well, I may be wrong. I dare say I am. Perhaps he wasn't *so* phoney.'

'He was exaggerating. Play-acting. That was all. Like

somebody playing a charade of what was really happening to him. It was his way of coping with his difficulties at the Moggs'. I thought he was a very spirited little boy,' said Miss Vaughan – and added thoughtfully, '– and a very angry little boy!'

'Angry ?' said Adam.

'Angry with his grandfather and his great-aunt,' said Miss Vaughan. 'Weary thinks he's been insulted with the half-sausage and the kitchen floor.'

'Well, there's not much he can do about it,' said Sandra.

'I think we may find he will do something, if it goes on,' said Miss Vaughan. 'Except that he appears to be very frightened of his grandfather as well as angry with him. And now ...' Dismissing Weary, Miss Vaughan paused and looked from one child to the other.

'The telegram,' said Adam. 'I've been eyeing it all the while we've been talking.'

'We don't need to guess,' said Sandra sadly. 'We know it's The Little Refugee Child at last. And it's no good us trying to pretend that we really want him, because you'd see straight through us. It is about him, isn't it ?'

Miss Vaughan nodded. 'It's from the secretary of the Refugee Association in London,' she said. 'It simply says that Paul will be arriving here on the 4.10 train from London. That means, I suppose, that he has crossed the Channel on the night boat, and will be reaching London this morning. He's with a party of children, all from the same refugee camp. They're in the care of one of the Austrian senior camp officials, who is, I gather, coming to England for his own holiday under the same hospitality scheme.'

'The senior camp official won't be coming here, will he ?' said Adam, horrified at the thought of any more refugees coming to spoil the peace of Long Meadow.

'I believe he is a most delightful man who has done quite

wonderful work for refugee children,' said Miss Vaughan rebukingly. 'But no, Adam – you are quite safe. He is nothing at all to do with us. He is only going to put Paul on the train at Victoria. And –' she paused again – 'I am going to ask you and Sandra to walk down to the station this afternoon to meet the train, and find a taxi, and bring Paul back here.'

The suggestion was greeted with silence by Sandra, and a low moan from Adam, who collapsed dramatically across the table and stabbed in a melancholy manner at the butter-pat.

'It would give you a chance to get to know one another on the way home. After all, although he is a Hungarian, he has been living in Austria. Almost certainly he will know Vienna. You should have much in common,' said Miss Vaughan, removing the butter, but making no concession to – or even visible recognition of – popular feeling.

'We shan't recognize him,' said Sandra feebly.

'There will almost certainly be no other young people alighting at our little station – if there are any other passengers at all,' responded Miss Vaughan equably.

'He won't speak English. Oh, I say. We never thought of that. I bet he doesn't speak any English.' Adam brightened at the prospect of such a debacle.

'Then we shall speak French – and, as you have lived so much abroad, I am certain you speak it fluently. It will be extremely good for us all to polish our French.' The small, trim figure that had presided over half the more aristocratic schoolrooms of Europe, rose inexorably to its feet, ignoring the groans from the refractory guests. 'And now,' Miss Vaughan went on, 'now you will want to be going on down to the stream, and I am going indoors to make a cake for tea.'

'What – like the one you did for us when we came?

With our names on it in white icing?'

'Just like the one I did for you and Adam. But this one –
naturally – will have Paul's name upon it.'

Miss Vaughan smiled benignly down at Sandra, as she
piled the breakfast cups and plates on to the tray.

As Adam carried the tray into the cottage, Miss Vaughan
proffered one crumb of consolation:

'You were saying, Adam, that you kept running up
against Greens. You've seen the pupils. You've seen the
owners. It will probably interest you to know that upon
your walk to the station this afternoon, you will pass
Greens itself!'

IV

'I DON'T understand why it's all so silent!' said Sandra.

The sun was beating down on the road to the station beyond the village. She and Adam had stopped by a pair of dilapidated gates, set in the middle of some fifty yards of creosoted fencing. Inside the gates was a short, unweeded drive to a square house, with a monkey-puzzle tree on its lawn. The house was smallish, of dark-red brick, and had an old-fashioned veranda running round three sides. It looked comfortable, sprawling, and neglected –

and was the only house so far that could possibly have been Greens.

'If it is the riding school, then why aren't there proper riding-school noises?' insisted Sandra, who felt cross with the afternoon heat.

'Riding-school noises? Riding-school noises?' Flapping a bracken-stalk to keep off flies, Adam testily urged Sandra past the gates, and along the road under the fence. 'What do you mean by riding-school noises? Girls shrieking "Whoa" and "Gee-up" and "Damn you, where's that Pelham?"'

'No, I don't. You know perfectly well what I mean. And Uncle Arthur said you weren't to say "damn". Oh, you are in a horrible mood. It's having to meet Paul. And you do have riding-school noises at a riding school.'

As if in answer to a challenge, the slumberous afternoon peace was rent by one long, high-pitched whinny from behind the fence.

'There you are!' said Sandra triumphantly.

'Well, I'll be blowed!' said Adam.

And then both children jumped. For, from the other side of the fence, with a quiet ferocity, a child's voice said:

'*I hate my beastly horse.*'

They turned wordlessly to each other, fascinated speculation on their faces. Then, together, they crept up the bank. Standing on tiptoe with their hands on top of the palings, they peeped over.

On the other side of the fence lay a cobbled stable-yard, backed by what was clearly a smallish stable. An elderly groom was leisurely crossing the yard, carrying buckets. He disappeared behind the stable without seeing the two heads at the fence. Sandra and Adam were not interested in the groom. Their gaze had fastened upon the small ring of four children squatting in the middle of the yard, leth-

argically scrubbing at tack, like a convict gang, with expressions of dreary loathing. There they all were – the riders who had trailed up The Heron Ride a couple of evenings ago. There was the fair-haired boy. Sandra's eyes rested on him. He looked older than the girls. He had long bony wrists, and his hair fell like a mop-head above a beaky nose and cheeks with patches of high colour, as if he spent a long time out in sun and wind. And there – Sandra's gaze passed round the circle – there was sunny little Ethne Blake. The sunshine looked a bit smudged off by saddle-soap and dislike for the job in hand. And there next to her, scrubbing furiously, was the pretty little gipsy-like girl, mouth taut, tiny gilt ear-rings swinging.

And there – looking as if she could do both with a man's hand, as Adam had proclaimed, and a good dose of Epsom salts, was the pudgy-faced, sallow girl with the pony-tail. She was sitting, cross-legged, all but strangled by the martingale she was supposed to be polishing, because she had allowed the bridle to collapse round her. On she went:

'If Dad and Mum weren't knocking round the Dolomites – or whatever you call them – on their lousy coach-tour, they'd come down and give old Mogg a piece of their minds. Last year, when the Greens were here, we all had heaps to eat – and even if we didn't look as if we were all heading for the White City, we had a bit of *fun* with the horses. Picnics all day – and – and *fun*. Oh, I *loved* Mr. and Mrs. Green. If I'd known changing owners'd be like this, I'd have gone to my Granny's. Look at me – half-starved and hardly seeing a horse, and when I do, we hate each other, great ugly brute!'

Her eyes fell on the fair-haired, serious-faced boy. She let out a snort, and gave him a sulky poke with a buckle. 'If you'd got any guts, you'd come with me and Eve straight to Major Mogg. If we all went together, and kicked up, we might get something done.'

'Coward! Coward! Julian's a coward!' chanted the small, swarthy Eve, crouching in a derisive way over her saddle.

Julian laid down his polishing rag, and looked at both ladies. 'I'm not a coward,' he said briefly. 'But I've told you it's no good complaining. This is a bad show. Something's gone wrong. And Mogg can be a bad-tempered man. I know because my father had him in his brigade once – during the war. Dad'll write to him when I get back to Wiltshire. But I don't want a scene now. He's in a black mood – and we can't stand up to his kind.'

'Not a man among us!' smouldered the pony-tailed virago, dashing her bridle down on the cobbles.

'Kah-h! *Boys!*' scoffed Eve, snapping a throat-latch with her fury. 'Don't waste your time, Sylvia.'

'Wait till Harry gets here. He won't put up with it. Harry's a fighter-boy.'

Sandra dug the entranced Adam, who was hanging all but head down over the fence. 'Look who's over there,' she murmured.

But Weary, hovering like a tiny shadow in the depths of the stable doorway, had already been spotted by the group.

'Hiya!' Eve's knuckly little hand had shot out with a denouncing jingle of bangles. 'There's great-auntie's pet, eavesdropping as usual. Who's got to sleep on the floor to make room for Harry! This place is a beastly swindle!'

'Oooh, don't be horrid to Weary!'

Charging herself up to play Wendy next Christmas, Ethne had scrambled to her feet, and was pattering down upon Weary with a wide, motherly embrace.

'Just you wait till Mum and Dad get themselves home . . .'

'*Just you wait till Harry comes . . .*'

In spite of Ethne's encircling arms, out of which Weary was edging in alarm, it looked as if he might need rescue. It came:

'*What are you doing spying over my fence? Come down at once!*'

Instantly the hysterical shriek quelled the uproar. A stricken silence immediately fell. Caught in the same embarrassing posture as Weary that morning, at the larder window, Sandra and Adam both shot round. Adam lost his precarious grip, and rolled down the bank. Clutching at her brother, Sandra caught her foot and fell on top of him. They picked themselves up, covered with dust, as Miss Mogg, shaking with bony fury, came rushing round the gate-posts, waving her arms like flags:

'Snoopers! Spies! Snoopers!'

And then she stopped. Shoulder to shoulder, Sandra and Adam confronted her in the road. She stood still. Slowly her features relaxed. A gaunt, anxious, elderly woman in a grey printed cotton dress, with an ingratiating smile beginning to stretch a face lean as a runner bean, she started nervously to apologize:

'I hadn't realized it was you! Miss Vaughan's little guests – isn't it? We met in her drawing-room. Still, you know, this *is* private property.'

Adam had just begun to apologize in his turn, when there came a further interruption. With a thudding of feet, round the gates and down the road, tore Weary. He performed a kind of jack-knife dive under his great-aunt's arm, thrust a sheet of paper into Sandra's hand, shouting, 'It's for you. I did it this morning.' And with his great-aunt in full pursuit, made off back to the house.

After a moment in the empty road, Adam said profoundly, 'They're mad. The whole lot of them – stark, raving mad.'

'You haven't got anything to eat on you, have you?' came Sylvia's hopeful voice.

Sandra and Adam turned smartly, and then did a backwards chassée across the road to get a better view of the line-up on top of the fence – three sad female faces looking down on them, like traitors' heads on Tower Hill.

'You're lucky not to be here, 's all I can say,' shrugged Eve, patting her hair coldly into place as Sandra and Adam shook their heads. 'You can wheel off the horses, for all I care. I'd rather be properly fed, if it's all the same to you.'

'My producer – *and* my agent – they're going to be ter-ribly, terribly cross, if I haven't learned to ride,' said Ethne, shaking her flaxen mop in an absorbed, bothered way.

'Yes,' said Adam pointedly.

Ethne blinked her blue eyes at him. 'You weren't watch-ing your telly –' she began doubtfully.

'The day you fell off the horse in that Western with the camera pointing at you – yes, I was,' said Adam heart-lessly.

'Well, poor child,' said Sylvia in a suddenly maternal voice, 'she won't learn to stick on it here. Major Mogg doesn't teach her anything. He's never here. Always over with his show-jumpers at some pal's place half across the county.'

'Only time we ever see a *horse*,' said Eve bitterly, 'is first thing after breakfast in the paddock, and that after-tea ride. And that's only because they need exercising. He just isn't interested in *us*.'

'Nobody's interested in *us*. *Nobody* cares,' broke in Sylvia passionately. 'Oh, and it used to be so lovely here. I came two years running, and Mr. Green got me ever so used to my horse, and I was never scared. And now we can't even pack it in and go home. Ethne's Mum's on tour in the north, and Eve's Mum's in the south of France and she doesn't know where her Dad is –'

Sandra stole a look at Eve, who was gazing fiercely and remotely out over the horizon as if she didn't care, not she!

'– And mine have gone off without me, and my aunties are all away too. Oh, well,' finished Sylvia without ran-cour, 'sorry to have bothered you, an' all that. Be seeing you. That was you, wasn't it, in that field the other even-ing? You looked just as if you was going off for a lovely gallop on that nice pony . . . I hate my horse – great yellow-toothed ole nightmare!'

As he and Sandra walked on down the station road, 'I hope she never does see you ride,' Adam, who spared one nothing, observed. And then he added, 'It's funny, isn't it, Major Mogg not being interested.'

'I don't see that it's very funny,' returned Sandra touchily, but wisely ignoring his opening thrust. 'I wouldn't be very interested myself in Sylvia and Eve and Ethne if I were a famous rider.'

'I would be in Ethne. It would be quite a thing to get that one to stick on a horse.' He began to giggle. 'You should have seen her,' he said reminiscently.

'I think they've all of them been frightfully unlucky,' said Sandra. 'Sylvia and Eve – I don't know about Julian, he seemed somehow different – but they are the sort of people who'd love the way the Greens ran the show, more like a holiday home with riding thrown in. And if Major Mogg really means to work the school up into the kind of crack establishment he had before, he must have been pretty bored to find he'd taken over Sylvia and Eve's kind with this summer's bookings.'

'And Queen Mogg is mean over food anyway –'

'So they come off badly all round.'

'And obviously King Mogg isn't going to bother about anything until he gets his school and his show-jumpers – there wouldn't be room for his own horses here – all up at The Heron,' said Adam. 'I should think things'll begin to sizzle then.'

'But it'll be too late for Sylvia and the others. Why do you think Miss Mogg came rushing out at us like that – all that shouting about spies and spying.'

'Mad. Mad as a hatter.'

'You don't think –' Sandra stopped, with an expression

of concern – 'you don't think she thought we came from that society that stops people being cruel to children? Because if she did, it means she feels dreadfully guilty, and really does beat Weary, like he said.'

'I'm not sure I wouldn't beat Weary if I had him,' said Adam. 'But I shouldn't think so. She seems the *mean* kind, but not the *cruel* kind. You've reminded me, though –' and he put out his hand – 'what was that piece of paper Weary rushed at you with just now?'

They had pulled up by an old stone bridge that spanned the Long Meadow stream, which had made an unexpected appearance at the roadside some few minutes after they had passed Greens, before bending away again across the open meadows. Sandra put her hand into her pocket and produced the sheet of paper.

Adam spread the paper carefully out upon the parapet of the bridge, and the children bent over it. At first the glare from the sunlight and the running water prevented them from seeing it clearly.

Then: 'You know,' said Adam, after a minute, 'it's pretty good. Weary can draw. It's a proper picture. See what it is?'

'It's us – you and Miss Vaughan and me – all grouped round Weary in Long Meadow this morning. That's just how we were,' said Sandra. She put her forefinger down on the paper. 'There's the cottage, and there's the gate, and there are the apple trees. It's a whole picture of him telling us his troubles, and he must have rushed straight home after we'd given him his breakfast, and drawn it.'

'It was drawn for you. It's a present for you,' said Adam. 'Do you see – he's got his hand tucked firmly in yours in the picture?'

Sandra looked pleased. 'So he has,' she said. And then: 'How tall and big he's made the three of us compared to him.'

'Well, dash it, we are,' said Adam. 'And the Moggs are even bigger. Think what it must be like being only as big as Weary, and up against *them*.'

Sandra found herself wondering if being up against the Moggs felt like being up against Uncle Arthur – and not only Uncle Arthur, but Aunt Lucia and all the cousins. Shielding her eyes from the sun, she peered more closely at Weary's little picture. 'There's one odd thing,' she said. 'We're all standing quite still, and bending over Weary. But he seems to be doing some kind of Highland fling. He's dancing on one leg and kicking up in the air with the other. He never did that this morning.'

'That'd be what Eulalia meant –'

'You'll call her that to her face, if you aren't careful!'

'No, I won't. But she said he was a spirited little boy. And that is spirited. Inside himself he was dancing a Highland fling to himself in the middle of all that jam he'd got himself into. You know – I know what he means.'

'I know what he means, too,' said Sandra. 'If you'd got to stay with the Moggs, and weren't going home soon like Sylvia or Eve or Julian or Ethne, you'd have to dance a Highland fling inside yourself, or die.'

They began to walk slowly and thoughtfully on down the road towards the station – a small wooden building, looking as if it were built on stilts, now looming in the distance. The countryside beyond the village and Greens seemed to have become more open and spacious. Curving away into the heat-haze, the Downs fell back to give the children a glimpse of the low-lying water-meadows that followed the course of the stream. There was a feeling of marshes, and perhaps – though a long way off – of the sea.

As they walked silently along, Sandra's mind returned to Weary's courageous little picture. It also returned to Uncle

Arthur. Perhaps Weary would have managed better in Bayswater than she had? Perhaps she, too, should have done some sort of Highland fling? But she was not that kind of person. Still – perhaps one should invent one's own kind of Highland fling? She shied away from the idea, and began to compare the horrors of the riding school Uncle Arthur had chosen with the horrors the Moggs were inflicting upon their pupils.

'What a waste it all does seem!' she said aloud.

'What's a waste?'

'Well, only there are all of them with plenty of horses and they aren't allowed to use them. And there's me wanting to ride and only old Toby, and I can have as much of him as I want.'

'Does seem a bit cock-eyed.'

'Adam – don't you *ever* want to ride?'

'Me? Me ride? No, I do not. Why, look at you all. Mad, the whole lot of you. I'd rather fish.'

They had reached the station. Nothing now, it seemed, could postpone the arrival of The Little Refugee Child. His train was signalled. They could see the railway line sweeping away in one direction across the open marshes, and in the other direction disappearing into heavily wooded country. Somewhere, through those woods, the train was even now descending upon them.

As Adam went up and booked the only taxi-driver in the station yard, a mood akin to despair crept over Sandra. Everybody – except Adam – wanting to ride, and yet everybody having such different ideas about horses! Ethne – only wanting to ride so that she wouldn't fall off in sight of her public! Sylvia – liking picnics but hating the horse she rode! Eve – coldly, dispassionately not caring a button!

And she herself?

She followed Adam silently into the booking hall. While he fumbled for coppers to put into the platform-ticket machine, she stood quietly behind him. Her eyes roved round the walls, plastered with advertisements of sea-side resorts. They all seemed brightly coloured pictures of piers, and deck-chairs, and crowded swimming-parties tossing huge rubber balls. *Sandisea!* Goodness, that was where Uncle Arthur had taken her and Adam and the cousins. That chilly holiday bungalow, perched on an unmade road, half-way up a cliff! If you moved an inch, tennis-rackets, golf-clubs and walking-sticks fell round you with a clatter!

But the poster which said *Come to Sandisea* did not threaten piers and rubber balls and Uncle Arthur's bungalow. It was different. Because some artist had used his imagination differently. He had simply painted a stretch of yellow sands – and perched on them a gay little merry-go-round, with children sitting on prancing white horses, which were whirling round, while the golden poles, twisted like barley-sugar, to which the children clung, slid up and down to music issuing from the centre of the merry-go-round.

Adam tugged and shook the antiquated ticket machine. Sandra stood patiently. Since horses were in the forefront of her thoughts, those on the little scarlet merry-go-round began to remind her of those other splendid horses she had once seen long ago. They made her consider some of the things she herself felt about horses. And they did not seem to be the same things that Sylvia or Eve or Ethne were feeling.

'The Horse,' quoted Sandra softly to herself, 'is a Noble Animal.'

She could not even remember where she had heard this – but she believed it. In her bones, she believed it. Because

of those dimly recollected other splendid horses that had
belonged to the good days before Uncle Arthur had dark-
ened the ways of her life, she believed the quotation.

Adam had nearly wrecked the machine. But at last
Sandra followed him to the ticket barrier, still pondering
The Horse. There seemed to be little possibility of riding
any other horse than Toby. She was lucky to have the
loan of Toby. Instead of day-dreaming about Horses with
Noble Natures, it might be better to get down quietly to
teaching herself what she could upon that reluctant bar-
rel in the Glebe. Imperceptibly she squared her shoulders.
Tomorrow she would start in earnest.

Nevertheless, as she walked on to the platform behind
Adam, she said – much as she might wish over a wishbone –
'Oh, I wish we could *all* learn to ride –' and added, 'those
of us who want to,' because she remembered that Adam
would prefer to fish.

She had not realized that the intensity of her wishing
had made her speak out loud. But Adam, peering down the
line to see the train come dashing round the curve, had
long ears. Over his shoulder he said very quietly and
kindly, 'Perhaps Paul will be able to help. After all, Hun-
garians are supposed to be wonderful riders.'

And at that moment, the train did come dashing round
the curve.

V

THE train came dashing round the curve with a roar and a clatter. It came bursting excitedly past Sandra and Adam, past the old porter who had come pottering out of the luggage room, past the little pink wilting rose-beds at the end of the platform, and drew slowly, slowly to a stand-still, sending up shuddering breaths of steam to blot out the calm, bright vista of marshland beyond the station.

'Supposing he's not on the train. Supposing he's missed it.'

'He'll be wearing a Continental suit almost certainly,' pronounced Adam, taking no notice of Sandra and scanning the length of the train.

For a moment nobody appeared to be getting off at all. Then, at the far end, one on each side of the restaurant car, two doors swung open.

'Look – look – that'll be him.'

In an agony of nerves now that The Little Refugee Child was really upon them, Sandra prodded Adam in the back.

'Yes – it must be. It *is* a boy. It must be Paul. No – no, it *can't* be! Why, *look* –'

Two figures had emerged from the two doors. The children's eyes passed rapidly beyond the little solitary middle-aged man in a macintosh, who stood, outside his carriage, gazing up and down the platform, to the figure beyond – the strenuous figure, half in, half out of its carriage, sternly battling with a suitcase jammed across the door. It was a boy all right. But – never, never a Hungarian boy! At that moment, the suitcase came crashing out on

to the platform, and the boy, seizing the handle, began to drag it at a run down the platform towards Sandra and Adam.

'He's in full riding things. Golly, he's got up for hunting. And on an August afternoon!' breathed Adam.

For one paralysing second, Sandra recoiled before this impeccable apparition straight from an outfitter's catalogue in brand-new jodhpurs, coat, stock, and velvet hunting cap, horrified that her wish might have been instantly answered, like Aladdin's, by a genie appropriately attired. Then, with the suitcase bounding and banging along beside him, the boy was on them. He was younger than Adam – a tough little bulldog, with square thrustful jaw, bulgy black eyes, and black hair so wiry that his cap was almost lifted vertically off his scalp.

'Hi,' he hailed them in stentorian tones, 'I bet you're from Greens, sent to meet me –'

At the dumbfounded surprise on Adam and Sandra's faces, the bulldog's own expression changed. The confidence vanished as though wiped by a duster. The bulldog looked mortally offended.

'Not to worry,' he said stiffly. 'They'll be waiting for me outside in the yard –'

Heaving the suitcase along, he staggered, head down, forcefully through the barrier, past the ticket collector, who stared after him, and out into the booking hall.

'Well!' said Adam, on another deep breath. 'What d'you know! Guess who –'

'I don't need to guess. I know. Fighter-boy Harry who's going to get Weary's bedroom, and whom we'd have got at Long Meadow, if Paul hadn't got in first –'

'Stone the crows!' said Adam, coming back to reality. 'That's just what he hasn't done – got in first. He really has missed the train.'

They looked wildly up and down the platform.

'There isn't anybody else, except that little man, and he's quite old,' said Sandra uneasily. 'Whatever can we do?'

'Telephone Eulalia,' said Adam, blissfully shifting the responsibility.

'But whatever can have happened to him? He only got to England this morning. If he's got lost, he won't know what to do or where to go. And I can't understand it – he was supposed to be in the charge of that man who was so wonderful right up to the last moment at Victoria.'

'Here, pull yourself together. Don't panic. We'll get on the blower right away. She'll know what to do. You just see,' said Adam reposefully, beginning to jingle the telephone money in his pocket. 'Eulalia'll cope.'

As the words left his lips, a light hesitant foreign voice behind the children made them both turn quickly:

'Excuse, please.'

Grasping a hold-all of red plaid woolly cloth, the only other passenger had come unnoticed down the platform, and was patiently waiting to claim attention.

'Excuse, please,' said the little thin man again. And then he smiled from one child to the other, a warm gentle smile that lit his honey-coloured face like Christmas candle-glow, and drew both children into its kindness.

'Perhaps you help? I have to find –' and the little man passed a postcard to Adam, upon which Sandra could see a few lines written in a spiky Continental hand.

'*Miss Eulalia Vaughan,*' read out Adam slowly, and then more quickly: '*Long Meadow Cottage –*'

'But that's Us!' exclaimed Sandra, and stopped. For the little man was beaming delightedly. He was shaking her hand, shaking Adam's – and even, while Sandra and Adam exchanged startled, horrified looks, stretching out a hand to the ticket collector, who found himself genially shaking it in return.

'All is well,' the little man was saying. 'I am indeed the guest who is expected. For one bad minute, I say to myself, "There is a little mistake. Onkel Anton is not expected." But it is not so? No? It is certain? I am wrong, then. And all is well.'

With a hypnotized expression, Adam dazedly led the way out to the taxi. He cast a longing glance at the telephone kiosk in the booking hall. But Onkel Anton was at his heels.

The taxi had not given up hope. There it was, still patiently waiting. But it looked somehow different. In some curious way, it now appeared to be bursting with people and luggage.

'But it's only one person, and one suitcase!' said Sandra in astonishment. 'Oh, it's – it *would* be!'

Leaning dangerously out of the taxi door, Fighter-boy Harry was helping the driver to tie his rocking suitcase in the front with a piece of rope.

'Hope you don't mind,' he called to Sandra, Adam and Onkel Anton. 'It's these people called Mogg. They wrote to my Dad saying I'd be met at the station. I said to Dad, I said it'll all go wrong. If you don't mind dropping me at Greens –'

Onkel Anton was already busily wedging his hold-all into the taxi. As he climbed in, Harry sat down with a thud, still muttering furiously.

'We *couldn't* have told him. What will Miss Vaughan say?' whispered Sandra agitatedly to Adam.

'They've sent someone from an Old Displaced Persons' Camp by mistake,' mumbled Adam.

Before the children could do more than exchange further hunted glances, as they settled themselves in the taxi, the driver – oblivious to everyone's crises – revved up. The whole party fell forward, sorted itself, and lapsed into silence. The taxi had started off down the long road to the village.

Soon they were bumping over the stone bridge, where Sandra and Adam had stopped to look at Weary's picture. The Downs were twirling into view, rolling and majestic. On either side, the marshlands were beginning to give place once more to meadows and hedges. The Old Dis-

placed Person had quietly settled in his corner, and was gazing out with an air of contentment at the peaceful English scene. But, having fidgeted since the drive began, the stocky figure at his side could contain himself only for a short while. Leaning forward, elbows truculently planted on knees, Sylvia's Fighter-Boy was single-mindedly demanding attention:

'Harry Burton's my name, see? My Dad owns that chain of garages – stretches all the way from Brixton to Bermondsey. Myself I prefer The Horse – same as my great-grand-dad. Never saw you about the village last year, or the year before!'

'You've been at Greens before?' said Sandra, for something to say.

'Was I here before! Why, Mike and I – Mike's my friend

only he can't come this year, because his cousin's come to stay – Mike and I are foundation-members! Why, Mrs. Green used to say she depended on Mike an' me to help her run the whole caboosh. I come every year – with Mike, of course – when Dad and my step-mum go to holiday-camp. But this year – well, I dunno quite! No Greens, and no Mike. We got a letter from Mrs. Green saying she'd been ill, and they were selling up, and hoping it wouldn't make no difference. I said to Dad, "Well, I dunno –" an' Dad, he said "Oh, give everything a try once, son," and my step-mum said, "Now we don't want *boys* with us, not on holiday" – well, fair enough! But I mean to say – no Mike – and them not *meeting* me like they said – well, I ask you, it's not a good start, is it?'

In the gloom of the taxi, as he paused for breath, Harry's stubby face suddenly looked lost and forlorn. But when Sandra quickly leaned forward to ask what Greens had been like, his expression of determined vigour was instantly back.

'Ter-rific!' said Harry. 'Go where you like, do what you like, eat what you like. Smashing! Ride all day – if you want to. And always plenty to do in the stable. I hope my chestnut, Penny, is all right. Mrs. Green said she regarded Penny as my horse.'

He fell silent, but only for a second. Then he asked anxiously, 'These Moggs now. You wouldn't know anything?'

Adam and Sandra were saved a reply by the taxi turning in at the gate of Greens. Harry slewed round in his seat.

To Sandra, if anything the drive looked less well-kept, the weeds higher, than three-quarters of an hour before. There was nobody in sight. Nobody was on the doorstep to welcome Harry. And the front door, with the stained-glass panes, was closed. She saw Harry's head turning quickly from side to side, surveying the tattered, unkempt garden.

'I expect you know Major Mogg's moving the school,' she put in quickly, 'I don't suppose they're bothering to keep things up when they're going up to The Heron so soon.'

But Harry's eyes had fallen upon the flower-beds. He let out a howl of grief.

'There's that bed I made for Mrs. Green. It took days. Look at it. Rack and ruin . . .'

It was unfortunate that, as the taxi drew up, a dim little trio could be seen through an open side-door in the wall, hopelessly crossing the stable-yard, tack dangling, feet dragging. Eve, Sylvia, and Ethne.

Harry's jaw dropped. 'Lor',' he said. 'They look like Holloway and the Scrubs knocked into one!'

As the taxi slowly backed into the road, and set off through the village for Long Meadow Cottage, Adam said darkly, 'I've looked in my tea-leaves. There's trouble coming from Fighter-boy Burton!'

'Miss Vaughan would say –' began Sandra, and fell silent. The thought of Miss Vaughan was sobering. She stole a glance at Adam, who helplessly returned it. What was Miss Vaughan going to say when she discovered that they had brought back from the station, not a Little Refugee Child, but an Old Displaced Person ?

Sandra looked at Onkel Anton. When the taxi had turned in at Greens, he had roused himself from his re-verie. He had looked alert and interested as Sylvia, Eve and Ethne had wended their doleful way across the yard. Now he returned Sandra's gaze:

'Riding ? It is a riding school ?' Onkel Anton said. And added, 'Horses ?', his voice dwelling on the last word as though he loved it.

T—c

Onkel Anton's face was like a bird's – keen like a hawk's. It had laughter-lines running up from the corners of his grey eyes. It was a kind face, Sandra decided. It was a *good* face. She smiled back at him.

'It is a riding school,' she explained. 'I don't actually ride there myself. It's too expensive.'

'You mean –' asked Onkel Anton – 'you mean, it costs much money?'

'Well, yes,' said Sandra sadly.

At that moment, the taxi turned off down the lane on the right-hand side. Sandra looked out through the window to see how near home they were. Then she began to laugh. There was the Glebe. And there, in the middle of the Glebe, looking more like a beautiful bulrush than ever, stood Toby – fat, lethargic, and gazing up in moonstruck manner at the sky.

'That's what I ride,' said Sandra, waving an arm light-heartedly at Toby.

Onkel Anton was looking out of the taxi window at Toby, as if he thought Toby was a good joke, too. Sandra's heart warmed towards Onkel Anton. He might not be a Hungarian Paul who was going to know all about horses, and make magic by teaching them all to ride. But at that instant she loved him, because he, too, saw that Toby was the most hopeless joke in the world.

'He is – awful,' said Onkel Anton.

'Yes,' said Sandra.

And together Sandra and Onkel Anton began to rock with laughter. She was just going to say. 'Do you know much about horses?' when the taxi turned off into the even smaller, rutted lane between the narrow hedgerows that led to Miss Vaughan's cottage.

There it stood – the white cottage, small, cosy, and friendly among its sentinel trees. Sandra remembered how

she and Adam had arrived, nervously wondering what lay in store for them. She looked anxiously at Onkel Anton. He had come a long way. Was he also wondering what welcome awaited him?

Sandra wanted so much that he should feel welcome that she leaned forward, and tugged at his sleeve. 'I *promise* you'll like Long Meadow,' she said earnestly. 'You truly will. Adam and I do. That's it. That cottage there. And under those apple trees is where we sit. And that's

Long Meadow beyond. And those are the cows. And those are the beech trees, and there's the stream where Adam catches fish –'

'I don't,' said Adam, adding resentfully, '*beastly* otter.'

But Onkel Anton did not seem to need reassurance. He seemed already to be quietly at home. He was sitting restfully, his eyes passing from the white cottage to the meadow, and from the meadow to the woods and the Downs. From wherever he had come, it seemed that he liked what he had so far found in England.

'There's Eulalia,' said Adam.

Round the corner of the cottage, Sandra could see Miss Vaughan carrying a cake from the kitchen to the wooden table, already set out with the tea-cups. She had not heard the sound of the taxi.

Sandra aimed a tiny kick at Adam's ankle. Adam said 'Ouch', but took her meaning. He flung open the taxi door, stumbled out, and started to run across the grass towards Miss Vaughan.

Sandra gave a small sigh of relief. Now Adam could explain the dilemma, and Miss Vaughan would understand. In her heart, Sandra knew that Miss Vaughan would understand – and that Onkel Anton would be properly welcomed. It was too much to hope – but perhaps he might never discover that he was the wrong guest.

'We're home,' she said to Onkel Anton. 'And that's Miss Vaughan. She's coming now with Adam.'

VI

ONKEL ANTON had climbed out of the taxi. Over his
shoulder Sandra had seen Miss Vaughan turn when she
heard Adam come thudding over the grass. She had also
seen a brief variety of controlled expressions pass across
Miss Vaughan's face as she spoke with Adam. Then, still
holding the cake, she advanced, a trim, erect little figure
in a pink linen dress, to meet Onkel Anton – with Adam
hovering at her heels, relief visible in the very set of his
shoulders. By the time Miss Vaughan had walked down
the brick path, Sandra could see no trace of any crisis upon
Miss Vaughan's face. Her free hand was graciously outstretched in welcome. Upon her lips was a friendly smile.

But alas, alas – although, as Miss Vaughan later said,
'My dears, we could not possibly have kept up the decep-
tion' – Sandra's hopes of welcoming a Displaced Old Person
instead of a Little Refugee Child capsized into instant ship-
wreck. In the presence of his hostess, Onkel Anton came
to attention so suddenly in the middle of the brick path
that Sandra nearly fell over him. He bowed low over Miss
Vaughan's hand outstretched for Onkel Anton to kiss – so
low that his eyes could not but light upon the cake in
Miss Vaughan's other hand. Onkel Anton's eyes rested
where they had lighted. Even when he straightened up, his
eyes still rested upon the cake. Adam's gaze had already
followed Onkel Anton's. Sandra travelled after Adam's.
Miss Vaughan, seeing three pairs of eyes riveted upon the
cake-plate, herself looked down. After a second's pause,
she smiled, and then laughed.

For across the pink iced surface, in a large flourish of elegant white-iced copperplate handwriting, skated the words: *Welcome to Paul.*

For Sandra it was a terrible moment. She could not see the expression on Onkel Anton's face, only the imperceptible sag of his shoulders. Adam told her afterwards it had changed to one of resigned dismay. But she saw him shake his head sorrowfully:

'I had asked myself,' he said sadly, 'yes, I had asked myself at the station, and in the taxi. Sandra and Adam – they were so kind, so determined to offer me the good welcome. But always there is the little look in the eyes – always it betrays! One is *not* expected ? No ?'

'Perhaps not entirely,' answered Miss Vaughan gently. 'But Sandra and Adam and I are going to welcome you as though you were. Although,' she added, 'I think we must immediately ascertain what has happened to the guest for whom we have now all realized that this cake was intended.'

And she waved the party over to the wooden table under the trees, as if she were about to supervise the pleasantest possible arithmetic lesson.

Sandra and Adam collapsed exhaustedly. Onkel Anton stood, still clutching the hold-all.

'There has,' he began helpfully, 'been the Little Mistake.'

As though encouraging a backward royal pupil, Miss Vaughan inclined her head, and said 'Yes ?'

'At Andelsbach, where is our camp, at the Bureau – they give us the addresses in England to which we are invited, and to Paul they give –'

'Ah,' interrupted Miss Vaughan, relieved, 'you know then the Hungarian boy whom we are expecting.'

'But, *gnädige Frau* – Madame – naturally.' Onkel Anton's hands shot out so wide that the hold-all had to be fielded

by Adam. 'Paul – he has been in my care – my charge –
since he came to the camp from the Vienna Reception
Centre – that is, since he came from Hungary as a little
boy. I have taught him with the other boys. He is charming – talented. Now, with his companions, I escort him,
for his first visit to this great country, England. . . .'

Light broke over Miss Vaughan's face. 'Then you are –'

'But – of course – I am Anton Weissman – Onkel Anton –
who is the senior camp helper. Who else should I be? I
have been many, many years at Andelsbach, Madame. I
have been at Andelsbach since the terrible days after the
war, when there were so many children in Europe with no
parents and no homes. I offer my services then, Madame,
after –' Onkel Anton paused, and let his gaze move, past
the group at the tea-table, down the peaceful meadow towards the Downs – 'after my own family – my wife, my
sons – were killed in the big air-raids. Oh yes, I have worked
in Andelsbach among children like Paul for a very long
time. Now I like at last to make my own holiday. I come,
I tell them, to England. And so they give me this address.
It is written down for me in the Bureau: Miss Eulalia
Vaughan, Long Meadow Cottage,' recited Onkel Anton.
'Here they tell me I shall be welcome. Here I am asked
for –'

'Oh, you are – you are welcome,' interrupted Sandra, her
heart much moved by Onkel Anton's story.

'Indeed you are,' said Miss Vaughan very kindly. 'But I
still have to pursue these inquiries, for it is I who am now
temporarily responsible for Paul.'

'About Paul I do not worry,' said Onkel Anton. 'He is a
most capable boy. It is clear that he has been given the
address in the north of England – in York – that I should
have had, for together we were in the Bureau when they
make the arrangements, and give us each the little cards.

I have a list of all the boys' addresses, and it will perhaps be possible to telephone the hosts to say that in place of the old, old man that they expect there will be a young, young boy – whom I have myself placed upon the train to go to them! And then tomorrow – tomorrow . . .'

Onkel Anton's eyes roved desolately round the garden, from the cypresses to the snapdragon beds, from the white gate to the hedge running between Long Meadow and the Glebe. His expression brightened. A look of recognition stole across his features. Hanging over the hedge was Toby's head.

Onkel Anton slid a glance of complicity at Sandra. 'He is there,' he murmured cunningly. 'He is with us.' The laughter lines crinkled at his eyes. 'I have had some little experience with horses as difficult as this gentleman. I could perhaps teach him to move quicker? I could perhaps teach Sandra –'

'– to ride!' burst out Sandra in such uncontrollable excitement that Adam groaned, and Miss Vaughan began to laugh at Onkel Anton's unabashed bribe to be allowed to stay among such charming hosts.

But Onkel Anton's future had to wait. For just then there was the clatter of distant hooves. With one accord, Sandra and Adam rose to their feet, Adam remembering just in time that he was profoundly bored by horses, and sitting down again.

'That'll be them. It's just about time for the evening turn-out,' he said languidly, with a wave of the hand at the Long Meadow gate across which Greens' cavalcade would pass up The Heron Ride.

'D'you think Harry'll be with them? Oh, I wonder if he's got Penny!'

'Well, he didn't look as if he meant to lose any time, travelling in full riding kit like that. They're coming a bit more briskly than the other evening, aren't they?' Adam abandoned the pretence of boredom, as curiosity took over. 'That sounds quite a smart trot they're putting up.' He rose to his feet, voice on a crescendo. 'Here they come –'

'There they are. There they go,' shrieked Sandra, pounding the wooden table as if she were cheering the Derby.

'There's Harry. He's leading. On the – yes, it is a chestnut. He has got Penny –'

'Har-ry! Har-ry!'

'There's Eve. There's Sylvia. Are they being bolted with? *Why, they're chasing Harry!* Golly – the whole show's got out of hand. Just shows what one person can do. I thought Harry meant business. That's what it needed. Come to think of it, that's what Eve and Sylvia seem to have needed!'

'Syl-via! E-eve!'

'My dear Sandra,' said Miss Vaughan feebly. 'What has come over you!'

Harry had glanced round, and instantly waved smartly. Hearing their names, Eve and Sylvia tried to follow suit, and nearly fell off. They disappeared round the bend, with Julian and Ethne following hard after.

'Where's King Mogg?'

'*There!*'

Thirty yards behind his pupils, King Mogg passed across the gate, sitting his dark bay easily, making his own pace, his own time. He might have had no stake in pupils or horses. The enthusiasm that had swept Greens had clearly left him unmoved. His whole pose spoke of superb horsemanship and supreme boredom.

'Jolly odd,' said Adam.

'He just doesn't care.'

'Jolly odd,' said Adam again.

A ripple of laughter from Miss Vaughan turned the

children's eyes towards Onkel Anton. Onkel Anton also
was on his feet. He was in the posture of one Riding The
Horse. Beneath him he had an imaginary saddle, imaginary
stirrups, and imaginary horse. With dead-pan countenance,
in rapid flickering succession, he was clowning an exact
but exaggerated parody of Sylvia, Eve, Julian, Harry, and
Ethne. Onkel Anton finished up with Major Mogg – the
famous international rider effortlessly displaying fabulous
skill to the unappreciative disappearing backs of the pupils.

'Oh-ho,' said Onkel Anton, finally relaxing and pretending to throw away an imaginary riding-stick. *'Schrecklich!*
They were – aw-fful! No? You tell me that is a *school*
where the pupils ride so badly ?'

'Really,' said Miss Vaughan, 'one feels most distressed
for those children. Major Mogg appears to be allowing
what has been a really delightful little small-scale holiday
riding school to go to pieces in a most marked fashion.'

'The boy who journeyed with us in the taxi – Har-ree ? –
he could ride well if he were not so headstrong. And Major
Mogg – naturally one would expect it of him. His name is
famous among lovers of the horses. I have myself seen him
ride. But the others! Nobody teaches them!'

Sandra and Adam gaped at Onkel Anton. Standing by the
wooden table, his cup of tea ignored, still gazing at the gap
where Greens had passed, his air of quiet authority was
unmistakable. The clowning done, Onkel Anton was
speaking like a king. Miss Vaughan was looking at him
with a sudden attention. She also had recognized the authority in the voice. For politeness' sake, Sandra and Miss
Vaughan hesitated. Adam leaned forward.

'When you imitated Major Mogg just then, you looked
as if you could ride like him,' Adam said quite directly.
'Please – do you know a great deal about horses, then ?'

Onkel Anton withdrew his gaze from the lane. The hawk

face curved into a smile for Adam. Then he put his hand into his breast-pocket, and produced a leather wallet. Out of it he drew a pitifully thin wad of paper money, and laid it aside on the table. Then came his passport. That, too, was laid aside. Then came what his fingers searched for – a photograph, the size of a postcard, old and faded. He smoothed its curled edge with care, and laid it down in front of Miss Vaughan. The children crowded behind Miss Vaughan to look down over her shoulder.

The picture had been taken indoors. It seemed to be of a lofty, beautiful and enormous hall, surrounded by two tiers of white balconies and columns. At the far end Sandra could see a great coat-of-arms over what looked like a royal box. From the high ceiling, in a blaze of light, hung glittering crystal chandeliers. But Sandra's gaze had fastened upon the centre of the vast hall. It seemed to be empty, completely empty, except for two small pillars erected right in the middle. To one side of the pillars a young man was standing, and between the pillars –

'I've seen a horse between pillars, back on his haunches – just like that!' cried Sandra. 'And in that place, too! That's the place I saw the horses. . . . I know I've been there. . . . That's where I went with Mother. . . . Oh, I knew I wasn't remembering wrong. The horses *were* indoors. . . . Oh, what a wonderful horse!'

'He is performing the *Levade*. That is one of the movements of the *haute école* – the great movements of our classical school of equitation,' said Onkel Anton proudly, tracing with his finger the superb crouch of the horse as it reared backwards in the posture of the *Levade* with its forelegs curved in the air.

'I do know that place,' repeated Sandra with rising excitement. 'Those galleries were full of people, clapping, and the lights were glittering and shining just like that. . . .

And there were lots more splendid horses like that. .... And I remember there were men in cocked hats who rode them round in a kind of formation. And I remember them all lining up at the end, and everyone clapping. But there aren't any men in cocked hats in the photograph. ... There's only that man with the horse in a uniform coat, and a squashy peaked cap. ... He's got the horse on a rein –'

'That's you, isn't it ?' said Adam quietly to Onkel Anton.

And then Sandra saw that the man, standing so proudly beside the beautiful grey, was indeed Onkel Anton – a young, erect Onkel Anton, whose face was stern with pride in the horse. It was the same face that now was smiling a little sadly at her.

'Where is it all ?' asked Sandra insistently, because her memories were now chasing her so hard. 'What is the place ?' she said, feeling she could not bear it much longer if she were not told.

But Miss Vaughan, who had been intently studying the photograph, looked up quickly – first, at Sandra with a smile that comforted and reassured her, and then at Onkel Anton standing by the photograph of his young manhood.

'It's the Winter Riding School, my dear. The Imperial Riding School in Vienna – the most famous riding school in the world. If your mother cared for horses, then indeed you will have been there with her, if you were living in Vienna. Everybody who loved equitation would, on some occasion or other, have been applauding from those galleries.'

Miss Vaughan turned to Onkel Anton, who had been listening to her in silence. 'I have lived in Vienna,' she said, 'and I have spent many happy hours in those galleries in the Winter Riding School. I know the old uniform of the grooms of the Imperial Riding school.'

She stretched out her hand to Onkel Anton for the
second time that afternoon. And for the second time Onkel
Anton bowed and lifted it to his lips. Sandra saw that the
tears stood in both their eyes. They were people who
understood each other's memories.

'So you were once a groom at the Imperial Riding
School,' she said, awed and wondering.

'It was so many, many years ago,' said Onkel Anton.

'And the horses?' said Sandra. 'I almost – almost remember the name of those horses. It was a long name – and it
began with L –'

'The horses are the Lipizzaners,' said Onkel Anton with
pride.

'That was it. That was the name,' said Sandra, her eyes
shining. 'Now I remember. It's one of the most famous
breeds of all, isn't it?'

'Yes,' said Onkel Anton. 'Long ago, in the sixteenth
century, Austria looked to Spain – to Andalusia – to send
her new blood-stock. That is why the Imperial Riding
School in Vienna is also known as the Spanish Riding
School. The Emperor imported the horses and started a
stud at Lipizza –'

'And the Lipizzaner stallions are all white,' said Sandra.
'I don't have to call the Lipizzaners grey, do I? Because
nothing could be whiter in the world. And they're the
most wonderful horses in the world –'

'Yes,' said Onkel Anton, watching her.

'And people come from all over the world to see the
Lipizzaners in the Imperial Riding School, and they all
have –' she paused, suddenly afraid of being laughed at.
Then she went bravely on, 'They all have noble natures.'

But nobody laughed. Onkel Anton nodded gravely, and
said, 'Many centuries ago, writers praised the noble nature
of the horse . . .'

At this juncture, Adam's eyes slid towards Toby rummaging in the Glebe hedge.

'Xenophon praised the horse,' said Miss Vaughan.

'So did Shakespeare,' said Adam unexpectedly. They all looked at him, and he quoted:

> 'So did this horse excel a common one
> In shape, in courage, colour, pace and bone . . .

'We learned it last term,' he said.

'Mother loved the Lipizzaners,' said Sandra. 'It was Mother who told me all about them. She went up somewhere into the mountains to see them.'

Onkel Anton smiled. 'She went to see the stud at Piber. The stallions are brought down to the School in Vienna from Piber –'

'And that's why I want to ride. That's why I'm going on about it,' said Sandra recklessly, not caring any longer if anyone laughed, or no. 'Mother rode beautifully. And I'd like to ride beautifully, too. And I'd like to see the Lipizzaners again. And I'd like to ride a Lipizzaner – even if I only did it once in my life –'

She broke off, because she was shaking with excitement – what with remembering about the Lipizzaners and discovering Onkel Anton had been their groom. And she recollected how the dream of being like Mother had grown during the years at Uncle Arthur's, and how when she was sitting in the Bayswater schoolroom among her noisy cousins with nothing much to say, she had often allowed her thoughts to dwell in that dream.

Fortunately Adam created a diversion by getting to his feet, and pointing up to the Downs.

'There they go,' he said. 'They've got there. Nobody's fallen off. It's just like the other night.'

Miss Vaughan went indoors to telephone to York, but

just like the other night Sandra and Adam, this time with Onkel Anton, went down to the white fence, and stood, shading their eyes, to look up to the Downs. Just like the other night, the cows were slowly moving up Long Meadow towards the Glebe gate, the shadows were lengthening, the colour of the leaves deepening, the same coolness and quietness of evening was falling over the garden. And, just like the other night, The Heron was tipped with flame from end to end, while King Mogg, with his riders, ran the gauntlet of the flaring evening sun, outlined against the sky as they passed across the high downlands.

'From here – from this distance – they look like the Lipizzaners,' said Sandra.

And, again, nobody laughed at her for her fancy that angry Harry, and sulky Sylvia, Eve and Julian and Ethne could look like the riders upon those fabulous horses.

VII

'You know – they really *were* going faster up The Heron Ride.'

'That was because of Harry. I told you. He was angry enough to get the whole thing jerked up.'

'You'd have thought finding Penny was still at Greens, and that he was riding her, would have calmed it off for him,' said Sandra.

It was early next morning – Sunday – and the two children were sitting in the dormer window of Adam's attic bedroom, with the morning sun beating down on their necks. The window looked out across the apple-tree tops over towards the Glebe, and down to the distant Vicarage. They had just seen the Vicar in black cassock, striding back to breakfast from Early Communion. In the middle of the Glebe stood Toby. There was no Sabbath air about him. Coming along the edge of the Glebe, Miss Vaughan could also be seen, hastening along the field path, also returning from church. She had on an old-fashioned squashed straw hat, with a lot of convoluted ribbon round the brim, and gloves.

'Wasn't Harry angry at not being met!' commented Adam, peering down in some astonishment at Eulalia thus attired. 'You felt in the taxi he wanted to push everything down. And Onkel Anton, sitting with his hands on his knees, was just the opposite.'

'Ah, he's not angry,' said Sandra contentedly. 'He's not squashing down his anger and pretending he isn't, like Uncle Arthur. And he's not letting it boil over the top like

Harry. He just isn't angry at all – in spite of all the sad and dreadful things that have happened to him.'

'There's trouble coming for Greens from Harry,' said Adam sagely. 'I said it yesterday, and I say it today. Those girls have found a leader! You just wait. You just mark my words. I give it a few days – and then something'll properly boil over the top.'

'It won't boil over on to Long Meadow Cottage,' said Sandra. 'And we've got Onkel Anton. Oh, weren't you glad when Paul telephoned him back late last night, and liked the family he'd gone to by mistake, and they liked him?'

'Eulalia didn't seem all that certain he did like them,' said Adam. 'She'd got a hunch she might have to be ready for him to change his mind when he'd been there for some days.'

'Well, so far he wants to stay. And they want to keep him. And we want to keep Onkel Anton.'

Adam grinned. 'Your luck's turned, my girl.'

'What do you mean? Oh, there he is. Crossing the Glebe. I thought he was still asleep.'

Adam laid his rod carefully across his bed. Together the children knelt on the window-seat.

'He's got Toby's saddle and bridle,' said Sandra excitedly. 'He must have been into the shed. Miss Vaughan must have told him about the Vicar lending us Toby. Adam, he's making for Toby.'

By this time Onkel Anton had approached within some yards of Toby, who was still standing with his air of aloof indifference.

'He's got a hope of making that one take any notice,' said Adam. 'Even a groom of the Imperial Riding School!'

But Onkel Anton continued to stand, one hand invitingly held out to Toby. After a few more moments of assumed disinterest, Toby shifted his near foreleg, turned his head,

and then walked over to Onkel Anton, stopping a yard short.

'G'lor!' said Adam.

'He's got the bridle on. He's testing out the saddle. Now he's tightening the girths. Now he's shortening the leathers,' reported Sandra unnecessarily. And then – oh, delirious thought – '*Adam, I do believe he means to teach me to ride Toby, even if he's not a bit like a Lipizzaner!*'

'And that,' said Adam, 'is exactly what I meant by your luck turning.'

After that, neither Onkel Anton nor Sandra wasted time making silly comparisons between Lipizzaners and the fat little English working pony. That clear, warm Sunday, and Monday and Tuesday mornings too, Onkel Anton taught Sandra so much – even standing still – that it more than made up for the dreary wasted hours at the riding school chosen by Uncle Arthur.

Sandra worked as hard as if the prize were a Lipizzaner, and something, too, seemed to happen to Toby, for he behaved with surprising amiability, not to say agility, as though somewhere in his dim, humble pony mind he knew how to comport himself in the presence of one who had worked in the Imperial Riding School stables.

By Tuesday Sandra had begun to find Toby interesting to ride. She began to enjoy using her own intelligence to persuade Toby to *try*. By Wednesday – though she would have died sooner than admit it – it had become more fun to be herself inducing Toby to trot and even to lollop in a canter, than to pretend to be imitating Mother careering round on a Lipizzaner.

'This pony,' Onkel Anton had pronounced, after he had narrowly watched Toby's response to the aids, 'this pony has once been a riding pony.'

And Sandra had leaned forward, and affectionately patted Toby's rough neck, much moved that he should – like the rest of them – have known better days, and even, perhaps, great days.

'Perhaps I could make him a riding pony again,' she confided ambitiously to Adam, who had spent three unsuccessful but blissfully uninterrupted days fishing by himself down in the stream.

'And what about the Vicar?' said Adam. 'He's not going to want his working pony turned, like Cinderella, into a fancy piece!'

To which Sandra surprised herself by retorting that it was time the Vicar bought himself a motor mower like everyone else, and Toby was partly retired anyway.

What with Adam absorbed down under the beech trees, and Sandra oblivious in the Glebe, there had been little time for meditating affairs *chez* Greens. Every afternoon Sandra had been so busy helping Onkel Anton mending, softening, and cleaning Toby's old tack that the whole Greens' cavalcade on The Heron Ride could have fallen over the hedge into Long Meadow without her being the wiser.

Thursday morning turned out to be another scorching day. Adam and Miss Vaughan had announced their intention of going on a brass-rubbing excursion to a small church in the next village. Miss Vaughan had cooked a large veal-and-ham pie, and put it in the larder to cool for luncheon at one. Then she and Adam had departed after breakfast, armed with long mysterious rolls of paper, and a horrible ball of wax, which kept dropping under the wheels of Adam's bike as he wobbled off, much hampered by the rolls of paper.

In the cottage, Sandra looked hopefully at Onkel Anton. 'It will, I think,' said Onkel Anton, 'be cooler in the lanes than in the Glebe.'

Under Onkel Anton's critical eye, Sandra saddled and mounted Toby. With Onkel Anton peacefully walking alongside, she rode him over to the gate that led into the tiny, rutted lane, at the other end of which stood Long Meadow Cottage. Once out in the lane, instead of turning back past the cottage, they faced left to potter up into the network of shady lanes on the far side of Long Meadow stream.

But as Onkel Anton shut the gate after Sandra and Toby, like Lot's wife, he looked back down the lane. 'There is a child!' he exclaimed. 'There is a child outside our own gate!'

Sandra turned in the saddle. Then she and Toby and Onkel Anton began to walk slowly back towards Long Meadow Cottage. Recognizing his quarry, Weary came towards them in a series of hops and skips. He slithered a glance at Onkel Anton, and ranged himself alongside Sandra. In the white sunlight, his small face seemed more colourless than ever.

'It wuz me morning walk,' he nonchalantly informed Sandra. 'I wuz passing, just passing.'

It was clear that Weary intended to accompany them, for he kept up, half-running alongside Toby. Most of the time he was silent. Occasionally he hummed a tuneless little ditty. Just when they were ambling gently along under the oaks in a lane branching off The Heron Ride, Weary embarked on a monologue so rambling that Sandra, preoccupied with all that Onkel Anton had taught her over the past few days, listened with only one ear.

She came to to find that Weary had transferred his attention to Onkel Anton – the ever-patient listener to small boys.

'. . . And me great-auntie, she said, "Drat all boys, since *he* come Saturday, they *all* want more to eat, perishin' cheek," she say. But me grandfather doesn't take any notice. *He's* too busy for that Harry. *He* doesn't take any notice at all, not till this mornin' – this – mornin' . . .'

Weary's voice had trailed unexpectedly away. It was obvious that this morning had brought something in its wake that had proved very disturbing to Weary. He was silent for a moment. Then he gave a little hop, and began to hum his airy-fairy tuneless little tune again. After a moment, however, he was off again:

'Harry, he come bustin' up to me grandfather. If Mike

was here, there'd be something done, so there would. And
why weren't they goin' riding more? And why couldn't
he have Penny? Why this, why that – Penny this, Penny
that –' Weary wagged his head, and ran monotonously
on: 'An' me grandfather – all of a sudden, he jus' *swore*,
and I see him seize his riding-stick –'

Onkel Anton was looking attentively at the little boy.

'What happened ?' asked Sandra.

'Dunno,' said Weary detachedly, 'I come for me mornin'
walk.' He had clearly been too frightened to stay for any
scene between Harry and his grandfather. He had, in his
own roundabout way, told his small story. It was off his
chest. He began to sing again. Then he stole a sidelong
glance at Toby. 'I liked the little donkey me Mum let me
ride at the sea-side,' he said covetously. 'I only walked
him. But it wuz a nice little walk.'

Onkel Anton and Sandra exchanged glances of complicity. Weary's mind had better be taken off his frightening thoughts. Sandra drew Toby to a standstill, and slid
off. Sensing what was in the air, Weary gave a delighted
caper, put his foot in Onkel Anton's hand, and hopped,
neat as a sand-flea, up into the saddle, where he said 'Gee-
up,' and broke into 'A-Hunting We Will Go'. Toby at
once took upon himself the character of any kind sea-side
donkey, and moved forward with a slow nautical roll.

They came soon to a fork in the lane. Sandra realized
that they were not very far below The Heron. She recognized down the side-turning a cluster of cottages not far
from the old Mill, and a telephone kiosk at the side of the
lane that belonged to the little hamlet. Just then she heard
a car coming round the bend down the hill ahead of them –
a car in very low gear and driven roughly.

Toby also heard the car. He stopped dead, with his ears
back, sideways on.

There was no danger, because when the car rounded
the bend, Toby was still some way up the road. Nevertheless, the car had to draw to a rasping standstill on the
gradient.

Onkel Anton was so busy persuading Toby to behave
like a gentlemanly Lipizzaner and shift himself, Sandra
so absorbed in watching Onkel Anton's handling of Toby,

that both jumped when the car door suddenly slammed, and heavy striding footsteps echoed across the tarmac. As they turned, Weary gave a pitiful little cry of fear.

Towering over them, stood King Mogg – his lean yellow face taut with fury. Ignoring Sandra and Onkel Anton: 'What the hell are you doing up here?' he shouted to his small grandson. 'You clear out after breakfast without a word, when your great-aunt wants you in the kitchen. Now I find you blocking the whole road. Here – I'm in a hurry –'

And without so much as a by-your-leave, Major Mogg brushed Onkel Anton aside, took hold of Toby's bridle, and led him to the side of the lane. Maddeningly, Toby went meekly.

'Now then – off you get,' said King Mogg curtly, lifting Weary out of the saddle, depositing him on the road, and aiming a light kick at his small behind. 'Get off home – at once – and make yourself useful.'

As Weary, his hands about his head, ran dementedly off down the lane, weeping, King Mogg had the grace to turn and begin an apology to Onkel Anton.

'Shouldn't have pushed your pony about like that,' he said. 'Lost m'temper. Fact is, a damn child down at my riding school had the impertinence –'

The apology had come too late. Onkel Anton had merely raised his chin slightly. Sandra saw that his grey eyes were like steel points. Then, with his voice also like steel, Onkel Anton cut straight across King Mogg's apology:

'Major Mogg,' he said, 'I have seen you ride in Vienna, and I think in Rome and Brussels. It was a great pleasure. But it is plain to me that, though you may well treat your horse, you do not know how to well treat a child, Major Mogg.'

There was a terrible silence. King Mogg stared at the

insignificant little man confronting him in the roadway. His hands went slowly to his hips. His mouth tightened. His eyes narrowed. Onkel Anton stared back at him.

Then – just as Sandra thought King Mogg would move in to knock Onkel Anton down – the unexpected happened. Abruptly King Mogg turned on his heel, walked across the road to his car, got in, and drove furiously away up the hill towards The Heron, with an angry screech of tyres as he rounded the next bend.

Sandra found herself shaking. Onkel Anton quietly took Toby's reins from her. With Toby between them, they walked down the lane to the turning that led to Long Meadow.

After a few minutes Onkel Anton observed calmly, 'I do not think that Major Mogg liked that I had seen him so magnificently ride in Rome, in Vienna, and in Brussels – and then that I should see him so lose his temper over a child.'

'He'd already lost it over Harry. But it was Weary that he went for,' said Sandra in a low voice.

'He does not strike me as a bad man,' said Onkel Anton thoughtfully. 'A stupid man in some ways – yes. And a violent man. But also a worried man. What is it, I wonder, that worries him that he must neglect his school, and does not treat well his grandchild?'

'Weary's terrified of him,' said Sandra.

'He is not happy, that little child,' said Onkel Anton. 'But I do not think that he is actually ill-treated. I have had much to do with children who have no good homes. He is an annoying little boy – as we might expect. They use him – certainly they use him for housework, and certainly they do not feed him well, or speak kindly to him. But one cannot bring the police to Major and Miss Mogg for this – when there is no cruelty.'

'I do hope his mother can soon, really soon, take Weary away from the Moggs,' said Sandra, almost in tears because of the small, jaunty, exasperating child who was so frightened.

Then Onkel Anton said, 'You mind – you mind, Sandra, that there are bullies. And that there are people who seem weaker that are hurt by the bullies –'

'Yes,' said Sandra vehemently, 'I mind. I mind.'

'That is all right,' said Onkel Anton peaceably, 'it is good that you mind. And that you yourself know what it is like to be bullied. One day you will perhaps do something against the bullies.'

'Like you did just now – with King Mogg,' said Sandra.

'I have had much practice,' said Onkel Anton.

They had turned off down the lane that led to the lower part of The Heron Ride, where it ran alongside Long Meadow. To take Sandra's mind off King Mogg, Onkel Anton began to talk to her about the Lipizzaners. And it was almost as if he took her away from the sun-scorched English fields to those clear meadows among the mountains, where the stallions and the dams and the brown foals that would one day be white, lived in freedom. Then he told her about the long three-year training of the stallions at the school in Vienna, and he described for her some more of the movements – the great movements – of the *haute école*. Sandra listened, entranced, to his stories of the famous horses he had known, recalling each by name – those horses who had excelled in this movement, those who had excelled in that. Above all, she listened absorbed to his tales of the magnificent stallion that he himself had loved the best, the one who, in Onkel Anton's eyes, had brought to perfection that most difficult of all feats, the *Capriole* – the great leap into the air parallel to the earth.

He was still describing the *Capriole* when they reached the gate into Long Meadow.

'Please tell me some more,' said Sandra, King Mogg forgotten, as she led Toby through the gate into the meadow. 'Please go on about the Lipizzaners.'

But Onkel Anton shook his head.

'We are both of us now at peace with the world again,' he said. 'And we have need to be. For now are our troubles again upon us.'

'What do you mean?' said Sandra.

Onkel Anton pointed up the meadow.

Sandra shaded her eyes. Sure enough, storming down Long Meadow, the cottage gate left swinging behind him, came Harry. Down he came, black hair pugnaciously upthrust, bulldog jaw out.

'I've been hanging round waiting for somebody to come back,' he called. 'You were the only people I could think of to help. We've all had enough at Greens. Hardly any riding, no stable-management, and practically no food. And now I've had a row with Old Mogg over Penny. He says he's going to sell her. I thought he was going to go for me, and if he had, I'd have gone for him. But his beastly sister – she had hysterics and started to scream. I've told the others I was going to telephone Mike; he'll know what to do. I said I knew you'd let me use your telephone. I waited until he'd gone off. He was going over as usual – leaving us with nothing to do – to see his beastly show-jumpers –'

'We met him,' said Sandra, with a reminiscent shiver. 'I don't think he was going off to his own horses. I think he was going up to The Heron. He was taking some spare halters. I saw them in the car. And he was in a terrible temper!'

But Harry was not listening. He scarcely allowed Sandra

to finish before he burst out, 'He says Greens is a *hole*.
When he lost his temper he really said what he was thinking. A hole! *Greens!* He says none of us are going to be any
good. He says he was swindled when he took over Greens. He
He hadn't realized it was such a down-and-out show. He
says Greens' horses are duds. Well, he knows enough
about horses. If he hadn't liked the look of them, he
shouldn't have bought them. He said – he said – *Penny was
only fit for the knackers. . . .'*

'He didn't mean it,' said Sandra. 'Harry, he didn't mean
it. He was just in a filthy mood. People say anything in
filthy moods. My Uncle Arthur says things. . . . Penny's
beautiful. Harry, she's beautiful.'

But Harry glared round him. 'All I can say is, Greens was
good enough for Mike and me,' he shouted. And in his voice
Sandra could hear a sudden fierce grief at King Mogg's
insult to the place and the people and to Penny, whom he
loved.

VIII

Sandra began to lead the way up to the cottage. Onkel Anton had basely faded out. She could see him in the distance in the Glebe. She feared that he would unsaddle Toby, and then plod on across the Glebe for his mid-morning chat with the Vicar, who plied him with coffee and asked him questions about refugees. There would be no more help from Onkel Anton.

'Mike's not half going to create about Greens,' Harry was saying, his bulgy black eyes angrily scanning the cottage as if the telephone might try to escape from him out of the window. 'And Mike won't let the grass grow under his feet. You see! I been saying to the other kids, "You see!" Now Mogg and I've had a real set-to – I tell you, Sandra, I nearly knocked him down – Mike won't hold it. He'll get on the afternoon train at Victoria, and he'll come. And then things will get cracking!'

'What do the others say?' inquired Sandra, perturbed at the thought of another fighter-boy of Harry's calibre arriving to support an enraged Harry against an infuriated Mogg.

'Those two girls – Sylvia and Eve – say, "*Go on – get Mike!*"' said Harry fiercely. 'Ethne – well, that doll can't think about anything except how many times she falls off. Seems it's getting fewer, but not few enough.'

'And that other boy? The older one – Julian?'

Somehow Sandra could not picture that boy with the calm face involved in all this excitement and bad temper.

'Julian? He wasn't there this morning. He goes off a lot

94

by himself. He went up into the woods this morning, after a badger he thought he'd tracked. He's not interested.'

They had reached the cottage gate. Harry pushed it so hard that it shot back on its hinge with an unaccustomed squeal of protest. Then he spotted his objective through the open door from half-way down the snapdragon path. In a second he was through the front door, and into the alcove at the back of Miss Vaughan's tiny hall, flashing the receiver up and down in a business-like manner, and saying 'Reverse the charge' impressively down the mouthpiece.

Sandra sank down on the settle. Harry scowled past her, tapping an impatient foot, and saying 'Hello there,' at intervals to empty air. Sandra wondered what she would do if nothing happened.

But something did happen. The telephone let out a click. Instantly Harry crouched down double over the receiver, as if it required cuddling. Swivelling hunted glances at Sandra – as if they had both suddenly become exposed to gunmen – he muttered, 'That you, Mike?'

With no warning, Harry then shot into an American accent while Sandra began to construct a picture of Harry's confidant, presumably also huddled over a receiver covered by gangsters in Brixton.

But quite suddenly Harry stopped in mid-air. The telephone had interrupted with a series of angry clacks. Sandra saw Harry's face change. It stopped being concentrated in fury. It became suddenly disbelieving – stunned – blank.

'A motor bike?' said Harry. '*A motor bike?*'

And then – in crushed tones with no American left – 'What had I *thought*? Well – I dunno, Mike. I sorter thought – you'd *come* . . .'

Clack went the telephone.

'We could give him the works together, Mike . . .'

But the telephone merely let out two laconic, contemptuous clacks. Then there was a ping that made Sandra jump. Harry shook the receiver, looking wonderingly at it. Then slowly he put it down. The stubby face turned to Sandra was bewildered.

'His cousin – he turned up with a new motor bike. He's been letting Mike try it out like, down a side-road. Mike used to hate motor bikes. He liked horses. But he said – he said – well, he just doesn't seem to have the time to come and help Greens. . . .'

He looked appealingly at Sandra. He seemed to be smaller, and he seemed lonely. She thought rapidly:

'Would you like a slice of veal-and-ham pie?' she asked, sliding off the settle.

Harry nodded in a daze. Like a boxer knocked silly, he followed Sandra into the larder. Then, torn between pride and the wish to be comforted:

'I bet Mike *wants* to come,' he said, biting into his slice of pie, and following closely at Sandra's heels as she led the way back into the garden. 'It's that cousin won't *let* him. But it won't be Mike if he doesn't come.'

'It sounded as if Mike were telling you to *do* something,' said Sandra. She spent the next few days regretting that reminder of those last contemptuous telephone clacks.

For Harry stared owlishly at her. Then slowly he sat himself down astride the bench by the trestle table.

'Yes, he did,' he agreed. He relapsed into solemn thought, one elbow planted on the table. Then he looked at Sandra again. Then he smashed his left fist into the palm of his right hand. 'We'll have to manage by ourselves,' he said. 'An' Mike's got the right idea. We can carry on –'

Harry broke off. His gaze went past Sandra to the corner of the cottage. He rose to his feet.

'Look who's here,' he said, with a nonchalant wave of

the hand. 'They've followed me,' he added proudly, morale restored.

By the water-butt, as if in a bus queue, stood Sylvia, Eve and Ethne. When Harry beckoned, they came tiptoeing across the grass.

'S'pose it's all right, us barging in ? Your Miss Whatser-name won't mind ?' said Sylvia uneasily. 'We got sick of mucking about with nothing to do, and what with being upset by Major Mogg swearing at Harry, I said "Let's go and see for ourselves what Harry's fixed up with Mike –" '

'What train's Mike arriving on, Harry ?' said Eve, in a business-like way.

But Harry was spared the embarrassment of an im-mediate answer. Sylvia had spotted the remains of what Harry held in the hand he had so graciously extended to his entourage.

'Is that pie ?' she said in a thin, yearning voice.

All eyes fastened bleakly upon Harry's hand. Then all eyes longingly swivelled towards Sandra.

In the brilliant sunlight, the Greens contingent looked oddly bedraggled. Sylvia's shirt looked as if her horse had chewed it, her pony-tail hung lank and uncombed. Eve's neat boots had long ago received a casual polish, her swinging ear-rings had tarnished along with what enthu-siasm their owner had possessed. Even spruce little Ethne seemed to have caught the rot. The blonde hairdo was hanging dispiritedly, back-combing gone with the hopes of sticking in the saddle. But it was the faces that touched Sandra. All of them – Ethne's bright and silly, Sylvia's, Eve's fierce and despising – all seemed downcast in the deepest shadow of dejection.

'Wait a moment,' said Sandra.

On her way to the larder, she hoped that Miss Vaughan

would be as reconciled to the loss of her pie as to the arrival of the wrong guest. Adam's reaction she put hastily from her thoughts.

When she returned, the situation had developed.

The girls were seated at the table, chins in hands, eyes on Harry.

Harry was erupting like Vesuvius. He was leaning forward, fists doubled over on the wooden surface of the table.

'We *gotta* do something.'

'Just a sec,' said Sylvia. 'She's brought the pie.'

While the pie was eagerly passed from starving hand to hand, Harry controlled himself. Then he broke out.

'Do you wanna do something, or just guzzle ?'

'You've had your pie,' said Sylvia, her jaws rotating round the pie as if it were ball-gum.

'Do anything you say, Harry,' said Eve, sliding a glance from under her eyelashes. 'When's Mike due ?'

'He's not,' said Harry. 'Important business. Detained in Town. But he said –' Harry drew an impressive breath, his eyes narrowing – 'Mike said, "*Get on and strike then!*" '

Mike from the saddle of the cousin's motor bike! Mike contemptuous, from his new eminence, of Greens! Sandra drew in her breath. Harry had reproduced faithfully the scornful clacks of Mike's last toss-off on the telephone.

'Proper strike does Mike mean ?' Sylvia was saying dubiously.

'*Proper strike!*' said Harry forcefully. 'Mike's Dad's a shop steward in the car factory where he works. He runs his trade union. Over and over again Mike's Dad's called his whole factory out on strike. Why, he – he doesn't even bother about it being a good cause.'

'We've got a good cause,' said Eve, coldly reflective.

'I said all along we needed a man to get things done,' simpered Sylvia. 'But a strike – I dunno. Major Mogg's a funny man.'

'Well, we can't go to the police,' said Eve. 'Nobody's actually starving.'

'The horses are in O.K. condition. He cares about them, cos he's paid for them,' said Harry, his eyes passing hypnotically round the table. 'No police'd ever take any notice of us complaining.'

'Teen-Age Strikes,' said Eve consideringly. 'They're all the rage. The papers are always on about teen-agers striking over school uniforms and make-up and jewellery.' Eve jingled her bangles self-consciously, her face set in lines of dispassionate thought. Suddenly she came to a decision. She eyed Harry. 'O.K.' she snapped. 'Anything to do something! *A Teen-Age Strike!*'

'How would we strike, Harry?' said Sylvia.

'Withdraw labour,' said Harry grandly.

'What – withdraw *us*? Mogg won't mind that, will he? We are withdrawn already. We don't get any chance to labour.'

'The horses are the labour,' returned Harry. 'That's what we withdraw. We take the horses away.'

'But we can't take the horses away from Greens,' said Sylvia, horrified. 'Where'd we take them? It'd be stealing.' She broke off: 'Ooh,' she said, 'here's Julian coming up the field. Coo-hoo, Julian –'

Julian had come up to the white gate. His face looked sun-scorched, and his fair hair was plastered to his forehead with the heat. He looked inquiringly at Sandra for permission to come in to the garden.

'I found a badger-run in the wood. I saw you from the other side of the stream,' he said benignly.

'Julian, we're going to have a Teen-Age Strike,' said
Sylvia.

'Better than hanging about,' put in Eve languidly.

'You want to strike, Ethne?' said Sylvia, seeking support
before Julian's silence.

Ethne had been turning her head from one speaker to
the next, her mouth a little open. She rallied gallantly to
what she had scarcely been able to follow. ' 'Course,' said
Ethne good-naturedly. 'Soon's possible while the weather
lasts. We none of us want to strike in *macs*, do we?'

'There you are, Julian,' said Sylvia. 'You want to
strike?'

'No,' said Julian, sitting down on the bench.

Harry, who had been barely restraining himself, thrust
his jaw out truculently at Julian.

'Why not?' said Harry ominously.

Julian hesitated. His long mild face was serious and concentrated. Then, quietly, he struck:

'I think it's a kid's game.'

'Well!' said Sylvia furiously.

'Who's kids?' said Eve with hauteur.

Sandra glanced at Harry, hoping that he might, with
grace, accept this candid judgement.

But Vesuvius was in eruption.

'It's not,' shouted Harry angrily, pounding the table
with his fists. 'Kids! It's not . . .'

And then came a dreadful moment. What with the
disappointment over Greens, the row with King Mogg, and
the new smarting humiliation inflicted by the odious
Mike, it was all too much. Harry's features contorted. There
was a horrified stirring among the ladies. In another moment, their Fighter-boy was going to be dissolved in help-
less tears of rage and grief.

'It's all right,' said Julian quickly. 'Have a Teen-Age

Strike if you want to. It's only that I think it's pretty dicey.'

'*Dicey?*' piped Ethne.

Julian addressed the whole group. 'It's what I've said all along when you wanted to complain,' he said steadily. 'You cannot fool about with a man like Major Mogg. Better to wear it for this holiday –'

'It's all very well for you,' interrupted Sylvia venomously. 'You've got horses – hunters – in that posh place you live in –'

'I never said it was posh,' said Julian, flushing.

'Oh, come off it,' said Sylvia. 'You can ride when you feel like it. This is our holiday –'

'I still think you'd better wear it, and complain later,' insisted Julian. 'Major Mogg won't take a joke –'

'There'd be no joke in our strike,' said Harry huffily. 'What would you get out of it ?'

'Well – I – I –'

'And what would you actually *do* ?'

'Yes,' said Sylvia, wavering before Julian's douche of common sense. 'What could we do with the horses, anyway ? I s'pose we'd take them when Mogg was over at his pal's place with his own horses. But we couldn't just leave them in any old field –'

'*I know what I'd do!*'

The tiny voice came from an apple tree.

Everybody jumped.

'Oh!' said Sandra. 'You were told to go home!'

Still tear-stained, Weary shot her a reproachful glance as he slithered out of the fork of an apple tree behind them. 'I didn't stay,' he confided. 'Not when I saw them come down here.' He eyed the group round the table one by one. Then – '*I know what I'd do,*' he sang tantalizingly, jigging from foot to foot.

After a pause – 'Go on, then. What would you do?' said Harry.

'I'd take the horses up to me grandfather's new house,' said Weary.

There was another long pause. Then Sylvia said grudgingly, 'It's not a bad idea.'

'It'd be *legal*,' said Harry with sudden enthusiasm. 'It's his own premises we'd be taking them to –'

'It's got proper stabling –' said Sylvia.

'But – seriously –' Julian had risen to his feet. He was looking worried. 'You can't seriously think you're going to ride the horses up to The Heron! What would you do with them? You can't stay there. The place isn't furnished. And you've got to eat. The horses have got to be fed.'

'Well, all we want's a Token Strike,' retorted Harry, bellicose once more. 'Mike's Dad's called out thousands of Token Strikes – people with placards shouting things. "*We Want Proper Food. We Want To Ride.*" And "*We Don't Want Penny To Go To The Knackers.*"'

'You told me he said Penny was *fit* for the knackers,' put in Sandra. 'You didn't say he was going to send her.'

But Harry brushed Sandra aside. His face was alight now, his brain racing:

'We'll ride the horses up to The Heron. Mogg's always with his show-jumpers in the afternoons. When he's back – an' we know when he gets back to Greens cos of our evening ride – then one of us goes and telephones him from that telephone box near The Heron. We'll tell him we've locked ourselves and the horses in, and if he doesn't do something, we'll jolly well let the whole village know we're there!'

'That's it. He wouldn't like that. Man of his famous reputation.'

'Might damage his new school,' said Eve thoughtfully.

'He'd like that even less. Who's going to want to come to The Heron if people are striking at Greens ?'

'Why, the Press might get hold of it,' said Sylvia. 'He wouldn't like that.'

At that moment Sandra happened to be looking at Ethne. As Sylvia's words left her lips, Ethne appeared to be seeing the most wonderful vision. Sandra heard her murmur, '*The Press!*' as though the vision were of herself riding, riding triumphantly through the gates of The Heron, Ethne Blake, Child Television Star, leading The Teen-Age Strike.

But just then Sandra's attention was diverted from Ethne's silly little rapt countenance by a disgusted exclamation from Eve:

'It's no go. We've forgotten something. We can ride the horses up to The Heron. But we can't get them inside. Those gates have got an outsize padlock on them, chaps. He's only had it put on lately. But I've noticed it every time we've ridden past.'

Sandra took a quiet step backwards. She would have liked to disappear among the apple trees. For this was where she could have helped them. Help them ? Help carry out one of the silliest ideas she'd ever heard of ? If Sylvia and Eve and Ethne had been present up in the lane near The Heron that morning! If they had seen King Mogg's face when he had encountered Weary upon Toby! There would be no such silly talk as she and Julian had been hearing. Nevertheless, she could not but remember King Mogg that other morning, hiding his spare key so carefully behind a stone in the Heron wall. And all the while she and Adam had been floating invisible far below in the Mill Pool. . . .

But, alas – 'Pouf!' said Weary, on a little strut. 'That's easy. Me grandfather's hidden his spare key under a stone in that ole wall. He thought I wuzn't lookin' when I wuz in his car. I could find the key of that padlock easy. Why, you can take the horses in to The Heron!'

And, at this fateful moment of decision, round the corner of the cottage, treading blithely, blithely for his lunch, came Adam, wheeling his bike.

Sandra forgot the Teen-Age Strike. She braced herself against the moment when Adam's eye should light upon the empty pie-dish.

IX

AFTER lunch, which had to be tinned ham, the children went down to the stream, with books. They lay half-way down the bank, just above where Adam generally fished, with the boughs of the beech trees curling beyond them into the water, and casting cool shadows over the pages. They were sleepy with the heat, and disinclined for reading. After a little while, they lay on their tummies and dropped small twigs into the stream, watching lazily as the water lightly swirled them down the shallows and away.

'Miss Vaughan didn't seem to think much of Harry's idea of a strike,' said Sandra at length.

'Who would?' returned Adam. 'If Harry himself had told her about it instead of you at lunch, she'd have shown proper disapproving. I bet he'd have abandoned the whole thing pretty smartly if he found Eulalia on his tracks!'

'Julian tried to stop him.'

'Didn't you do *anything* – except give away our pie?'

'I wasn't in the picture,' said Sandra. 'You've no idea how left out I was – once Eve and Sylvia and Ethne had clutched on to Harry's idea. They've become a very *tight* little bunch – those Greens people. It's having so much to grouse about –'

Adam laughed. 'They're getting like a lot of hardened old soldiers, always grumbling and never doing – except that this time they really do mean to do something. Still, I'd have thought Julian could have put a stop to it. I never can quite make out what Julian's doing at Greens, anyway.

He doesn't seem to belong in the least. And I don't believe he's really interested in horses.'

Sandra reflected for a moment. Then a silent streak of movement across the deep water downstream caught her eye. She put out a hand to Adam. Together they watched the swift, thrusting passage of a water-rat from the hanging undergrowth to the opposite bank.

'Julian *is* different,' she said, when the water-rat had disappeared. 'He's –' she sought for a description of Julian – 'he's a *composed* person,' she said, and added, 'all the others rush about so, and get worked up –'

'It's too *hot* to get worked up,' mumbled Adam sleepily, dropping his head down on to his arms with a large yawn.

This time there was a long silence, with no sound but a cow chewing near by.

Then Sandra rolled over to face Adam. 'I do wish,' she said, 'I do wish Harry wasn't dragging them all into this thing.'

Adam said nothing. He might have been sound asleep.

'They won't get anything out of it. King Mogg won't like being made a fool of, and he's not likely to turn nice suddenly. People never seem to. And supposing there is trouble, and he does lose his temper and knock one of them about –'

'Did you say they were going to lock themselves in The Heron so that he couldn't get at them ? Isn't he supposed just to be going to shout and rave from the road outside ?' came Adam's voice, muffled by his arms.

'Well, who wants him shouting and raving anyway ? They don't seem to realize how beastly it is having people shouting and raving. It'll all be horrible anyway – whatever happens. Suppose King Mogg just expels the lot – like a proper school. Nobody's parents are get-at-able – except Julian's. Why, Eve doesn't know where her father is. Her parents are divorced. And Sylvia's people have gone off without her. And Harry's stepmother doesn't like boys when she's on holiday. She wouldn't want Harry suddenly landed on her, and you know how funny he is about not being wanted. And Ethne's mother's an actress and is acting madly up in the North —'

'For heaven's sake, shut up. I shall be in tears in a moment,' said Adam. 'I should think Ethne's producer and her agent would go into a dissolve if they knew how much horsemanship Baby Brighteyes was learning. She ought to be able to fall off both sides in her next Western.'

'Harry says she's improving,' said Sandra absently. Then she burst out, 'The whole thing's just plain babyish, and if Eve and Sylvia weren't bored they'd never follow Harry like this. He's making them all behave like children in an adventure story — only King Mogg isn't in a story, and he won't do what they think he ought to. He's *real* — horribly *real*.'

Adam raised his head, and regarded Sandra. 'You are interested in them all of a sudden, aren't you!' he commented. 'It's nothing to do with us, you know. We're here to have a highly-deserved holiday at Long Meadow Cottage. We don't have to bother ourselves with what's going on at a riding school down the road.'

Sandra sat up, and stared at him. 'You hideous prig!' she said. 'Even if it isn't anything to do with us — I am interested — I mind about —'

She minded about Weary — small, angry, defiant. She minded about Harry, because he, too, was hurt and angry and desperate. Eve — who was jauntily reckless. Sylvia — sulky with disappointment. They were all people who had been sent to Greens because other people had not wanted them. And Greens had failed them. Before, there had always been a welcome. She remembered Miss Vaughan in the dining-room last week at tea-time, talking about the refugees she had seen in Vienna. 'They didn't belong any-where,' Miss Vaughan had said. Julian and Ethne were all right – they had their own reasons for coming to Greens. But Sylvia, Eve, Weary, and Harry – they didn't seem to belong anywhere. She had forgotten that she had said the same thing of herself to Adam on this very spot down in Long Meadow.

'I do mind –' she repeated.

'All right. All right,' said Adam. 'Come to that, so do I mind. And I know what's worrying me, too. One – how are they proposing to get the horses away from Greens without *both* Moggs out of the way? You remember how quickly Queen Mogg was on to us when we were looking over the fence, and she thought we were up to some-thing.'

'I don't think they'd got as far as that,' said Sandra. 'What's the second worry?'

'Only how are they proposing to lock themselves inside The Heron? Has the place got bolts *inside* the gates as well as a padlock *outside*?'

'They were babbling on about locking themselves in when you were putting your bike away,' said Sandra. 'Then you appeared, and they stopped. Nobody mentioned bolts at all.'

'All I can say is that I think the whole thing stinks!' announced Adam elegantly. 'And I'm with you. Mogg could turn thoroughly nasty.'

'Like he did on the road with Weary, this morning,' said Sandra. 'Onkel Anton was wonderful.'

At that moment, a cow shuffled restlessly in the grass beyond the shelter of the beeches. Adam drew the branches aside.

'It's Eulalia,' he said.

Miss Vaughan was coming down Long Meadow, looking cool under a large linen sunshade lined with green, and carrying two towels and her own embroidery bag.

'The sun will be moving off the Mill Pool soon, and you may find it a little chilly,' she observed.

The children scrambled to their feet. Miss Vaughan handed over the towels, and settled herself comfortably against the trunk of a beech tree.

'I was telling Adam that Onkel Anton was wonderful this morning,' said Sandra. 'He really stood up to King Mogg. King Mogg looked as if he were going to knock Onkel Anton down.'

Miss Vaughan smiled up at both children.

'He is a brave man, my dears. And a very wise and kind man. The refugee camp at Andelsbach is very fortunate in having him.'

'He seemed to know what it was like being Weary and being bullied,' said Sandra. She added gratefully to herself, 'He seemed to know, too, what it was like being me!'

The children slung the towels round their necks, and started along the bank for the Mill Pool, leaving Miss Vaughan placidly embroidering in the shade, surrounded by cows.

It was some days since they had been to swim in the pool. Beyond the spinney and the two fields, the hot weather had shrunk the stream into its bed even further. The mud on the banks had dried harder still, so that the narrow passage was easier than the first morning.

Sandra's thoughts were still revolving around Miss Vaughan and Onkel Anton. When Adam paused for breath, leaning back against a giant oak, she said diffidently, 'Have you noticed how like being with them is to being back with Father and Mother ?'

Adam said nothing. But Sandra did not find his silence

discouraging. She went on: 'I think it's mostly the conversation. Somehow at Uncle Arthur's it was either bickering – or never about anything very much. But with them, it's always about things –'

'And it's often funny. We laugh a lot here,' said Adam.

Feeling much in accord with Adam, Sandra followed him closely as he went ahead, holding back the trailing undergrowth for her. The wood was now closing darkly around them, with sparkles of light upon the narrow ribbon of stream. As they walked farther into its depths, she went on thinking about Long Meadow Cottage – and then about Father and Mother, and the houses they had lived in that were so different from Long Meadow, and yet so like. For the first time in four years, the memories of the Beautiful Cities did not seem so sad. They seemed, in fact, rather gay. She began to remember the jokes that Father and Mother used to make. They had been good jokes, funny family jokes – jokes such as she and Adam and Miss Vaughan and Onkel Anton were now always making. She wondered how Mother and Father would have liked Miss Vaughan and Onkel Anton. Father would have enjoyed Miss Vaughan's dry common sense, and humour, and learning. They were both learned people – as Adam was. Mother and Onkel Anton could have talked about the Lipizzaners, and the stud that they both had visited up in the mountains. It was a pity that all these people who would have liked each other, and enjoyed each other's company, would not meet in this life. 'Oh, you old *Death*!' she said to herself, as they went on through the deepening wood.

Presently they clambered over the last difficult tree-trunk, rounded the last corner – and there lay the Mill Pool, less alluring than usual, because the sun was indeed passing across the tree-tops, and half the water already lay in black shadow. But high up the slope on the opposite side, The Heron was still standing in golden light.

'You know,' said Adam, as they undressed in the shadow of the Mill, 'I was thinking just now about that question of bolts. They'll need every bolt they can get between them and King Mogg until he cools down. I wonder if those gates –' and he waved in the direction of The Heron – 'really are fitted with bolts.'

'Well, I don't suppose they'll ever think to check,' said Sandra. 'After all, none of them will walk as far as The Heron, and they can't dismount when they ride past with King Mogg.'

There was a splash. Adam had dived into the pool. He surfaced, swam out to the middle, turned, and came back to talk to Sandra, who was still hovering on the brink.

'When we're dry,' he said, 'we could climb up to The Heron, and have a look.'

With a little gasp at the chill of the water, Sandra slid into the pool. She swam out towards the sunlight, Adam trudging alongside.

'How could we tell?' she said. 'The gates are padlocked.'

Then she stopped swimming. 'Oh, I see what you mean,' she said faintly. 'You mean –'

'Yes. We can look for that spare key behind the stone.'

'But suppose King Mogg comes. We know he does come up to The Heron –'

'But this is the one time he won't,' said Adam triumphantly. 'By the time we've dried off, and had a sit in the sun, it'll be just about time for Greens to be passing on the way up to the Downs. All we've got to do is climb up that slope, watch for the whole lot to go tearing past, and then nip across the road, have a shot at finding the key, and if we're lucky, we can have a quick look at the inside of the gates. It won't take two minutes to see if they're fitted with bolts. And I'd feel a lot easier if I knew they were.'

'And if they aren't?'

'Then we'll have to think again. Try and get hold of Julian and get him to knock some sense into Harry, probably.'

It all sounded simple. But Sandra swam back to the bank with considerably diminished enthusiasm.

They sat in the sun for some little while, with the towels spread out to dry. Then Adam looked at his watch, and they scrambled up the steep slope among the tree-trunks, hauling themselves up by the low branches, and finding footholds among outgrowing roots.

'We simply must not be seen,' said Adam, looking round for cover. 'Except for Julian, they're all so silly that they'll almost certainly wave and shriek at us as they pass.'

They had hardly settled themselves down on the dried moss behind a clump of bushes opposite The Heron, when they heard the now familiar clip-clop of horses' hooves further down the hill. They crouched lower as the Mogg contingent came trotting briskly round the bend.

The cavalcade seemed to be in better order than on the night of Onkel Anton's arrival. Harry was again in the lead, an impression of dramatic urgency imparted by hunched shoulders and hands low on Penny's neck. Penny appeared to be going strongly and easily – certainly no case for the knackers! Eve and Sylvia once again looked as if they were in competitive pursuit of Harry, Eve's roan edging Sylvia's light bay towards the side of the road, the latter unpleasantly showing his teeth in the yellow grin disliked by Sylvia. Behind them, bouncing jerkily, tipping forward, but sticking it manfully, came Ethne, scarlet with worried concentration. They all swung round the next bend of the cork-screw, with King Mogg bringing up the rear as usual on his powerful dark bay.

'They looked better,' said Sandra, brushing herself free of dried twigs and moss.

'That's knowing they're going to strike,' said Adam wisely. 'Nothing like having a plan for pulling everyone together!'

'Sylvia was riding pretty short, wasn't she!' commented Sandra. 'And as for Eve – well, you could see the hill between her knees – and as for Ethne –'

To which Adam, now openly surveying The Heron from the middle of the road, returned, 'I knew you'd soon begin to show off!'

'Well,' said Sandra hurriedly, incapable of fielding this ball because it was accurately aimed, 'well, why do you think Julian wasn't there?'

'Wasn't he?' said Adam absently.

'No, he wasn't. Adam, what d'you think's happened to Julian?'

'No idea,' said Adam, uninterested. 'Look here,' he went on from the middle of the road, pursuing what was in his mind. 'I don't know about getting that key from the wall. What do you think about making a tour round the entire wall first? I hadn't realized till I looked down there –' pointing to where the wall began to run down the left-hand side of the Heron garden – 'that it doesn't go all the way round the garden. It becomes a fence much lower down. It's not going to be much use even if there are bolts on the gates, if Mogg can quite easily get over the garden fence.'

They began slowly to skirt the wall of the house, walking down through the woodland on the north side, and looking up at the tall old grey stone wall that enclosed the property. It was a wall well built to keep out intruders, with old-fashioned pieces of dirty broken glass stuck closely along its top.

'King Mogg couldn't climb over that,' said Sandra. 'Not unless he was an acrobat who was going to swing in from the tree-tops!'

But pretty soon – as Adam had observed from the road – the wall stopped, and joined an equally high fence, with two rusty strands of barbed wire running along the top. The trees were pressing close up to the fence, and the children had to edge their way along a deep, dry ditch lined with dock and nettles.

'They're perfectly safe,' Sandra had just said. 'Nobody could really get over this fence – no more than the wall.'

And then she stopped.

Adam was pointing to the fence some few yards ahead.

'There's a hole,' he said. 'Nobody's bothered to crawl along this ditch to mend it, even if it's been spotted. It's almost too low to see, anyway.'

'He couldn't get in by that,' said Sandra. 'No grown-up could. Only a child, and a very small child. Oh, Adam –' and she gave a little yelp – 'Adam, what are you doing? *Come back!*'

For Adam had ducked down at the hole, given a little wriggle, and, with a sound of rotten splintering wood, disappeared through the now much larger hole into the Heron garden.

'Adam – come out,' implored Sandra, left alone in the wood. 'Come out – Adam – Adam –'

'I'm not going to come out,' said Adam's voice from the other side of the fence. 'And you'd better come through yourself. We can go up the garden, and have a look at those bolts from the inside.'

X

THE Heron garden was very large. It was very wild, and very green – green with a tangle of apple trees, unpruned for so long that their branches bowed down to the earth, and green with undergrowth beyond the trees, that no hand had for many years cut back. The apple trees seemed to stretch away, away into the distance. But between them Sandra could just discern something towards the centre of the garden that looked quite different. There seemed to be lines of long alleys, bordered by high hedges, converging upon – what?

'I think I know,' said Adam quietly, breaking the warm, heavy silence that hung over The Heron. He began to walk stealthily down between the apple trees, and on down the straight green alley beyond. Suddenly he gave a small murmur of satisfaction.

'I wondered if it would be about here,' he said. 'I didn't think I'd got it wrong. I remembered Eulalia saying . . .'

There in front of them, with four grass alleys converging, lay a stone-rimmed pool, covered with water-lily leaves, and in the middle, on a tiny old stone pedestal, green with age and the years of sun and rain, stood a small leaden bird.

'It's the heron,' whispered Sandra.

Together they moved softly to the rounded rim of the stone basin, and gazed at the little heron where it stood, with every detail of its wings, its faint plumage, its raised long beak faithfully reflected in the still, dark water between the lily leaves.

It looked as if it had always been there, as if the garden had grown up around it – the tiny replica of the heron that, all those years ago, had flown up from the marshes to this alien garden, and so accommodated himself that always he was at home, and always when he went away, returned.

'Why is the heron like Onkel Anton?' said Sandra, as if she were asking a riddle.

'Why is he?' said Adam, still staring at the little leaden heron.

'Because *he* is at home, wherever he goes,' said Sandra wistfully.

They walked ceremoniously twice round the pool, and then turned up that grass alley which led towards the house. At its end, the vista opened before them of a wide lawn, and beyond the lawn a grey stone terrace running

the length of the house, which looked larger than from
The Heron Ride. The terrace had a flight of broad shallow
steps leading up to it, with a curving balustrade, flanked
at the bottom by old stone urns, spilling over with a falling tangle of leaves.

At the foot of the steps, Adam paused. He gazed up at
the long line of windows. Then he turned and looked back
over the garden – back over the lawn, to the grassy alleys,
and beyond to the wild, heavy tangle of summer roses and
trees.

'Some day,' he said thoughtfully, 'some day I shall buy
this house. You remember what I said in Long Meadow
the other day? That when Uncle Arthur had finished
educating us, we would say "thank you" and go, and that
we would buy our own house. Well, this is it. This is the
house. We've found it sooner than we thought.'

Sandra looked up at the grey house. 'I hope King Mogg
spends some money on paint,' she said. 'Before he retires,
and we take it on, I mean. It's in a bad state.'

'I hope he doesn't get ideas about the garden,' said
Adam. 'Beyond clipping the hedges, and the lawn, and
some pruning.'

He began to walk slowly up the middle of the flight of
steps.

'Actually,' he said casually over his shoulder, 'this
garden reminds me a bit of one of our gardens – the one
in Vienna.'

And to Sandra – who had been wondering how much
Adam remembered – this remark came as a reassurance
that between them would always be the memories shared.
At that moment, she knew that if Adam wanted to buy
The Heron, it was not only to get them both away from
Uncle Arthur. It was because he also loved what had
been lost – although, she thought sorrowfully, he seemed

to have managed better than she, who had let herself
become so unhappy. . . .

They had both forgotten that they were trespassers, and
upon what errand they had come. They dawdled down
the terrace, peeping through the grimed french windows
into the large empty rooms on the ground floor of the
house. It was Sandra who recollected herself first:

'Adam,' she said, as if waking up from a good dream,
'Adam, oughtn't we to –'

'Yes,' said Adam, 'we ought. Those buildings'll be the
stables.'

He indicated a group of outhouses to the right of the
house, beyond the wall that ran across between them and
the front of The Heron. There was a door open in the
wall on the left-hand side which brought them out in the
drive, and within a minute they had passed the front door
and found the group of buildings.

It was now easy to see why Major Mogg had considered
The Heron suitable for expanding Greens into a large
riding establishment. For the people who had added to
the old house in the last century must themselves have
loved horses. The stables that surrounded the vast court-
yard giving off the drive and facing the gates looked large
and capacious. They were topped by a stable clock and a
green cupola. Adam stood looking, not at the stables, but
at the big double gates at the end of the short drive.

'Those are our gates all right,' he said. 'Outside there is
The Heron Ride. And –' he turned back to Sandra – 'do
you see what I see ?'

'Large, heavy, brand-new bolts,' said Sandra. 'Top and
bottom.'

'So we needn't bother ourselves any more,' said Adam.
'If they are silly enough to stage a strike, and King Mogg
does come after them, he can't just push the gates open –'

'*What's that noise?*' said Sandra.

'Now it's quite all right,' began Adam soothingly. 'You know quite well he's up on the Downs on a horse. And that's a car. And in another second you're going to hear it go tearing past up the hill –'

'I'm not going to hear it go tearing past up the hill,' interrupted Sandra in a small voice, 'because it's stopping outside the gates. And, Adam, *the gates may have bolts, but they aren't bolted!*'

But Adam had already seized Sandra's elbow, and was propelling her across to one of the open half-doors of the stable. He pushed her into the dark interior, pulled to the lower half of the door, and then watched from the inside of the stable.

'It can't – it still can't be King Mogg,' he whispered reassuringly.

They heard the click of the key in the padlock, the padlock scrape as it was withdrawn, and the handle of the great gates rattle as it was turned. Then the left-hand gate shook as somebody eased it back, scraping it rapidly across the gravel in the drive. To the surprise of Sandra and Adam, a fat, chubby-faced man in a town suit appeared in the entry. He held the padlock in one hand, and a folded carpenter's rule in the other.

'I've seen that man about the village,' murmured Adam. 'He's Mr. Wyborn. He comes about people's houses being decorated. He was round at the cottage one morning when you were down by the stream. He comes out from a firm of decorators in Ardsham – that's that town Miss Vaughan goes to for shopping.'

Mr. Wyborn had skipped to one side, and was beckoning. A small car swept jerkily round the gate-posts, up the drive, and pulled up with a bounce outside the front door. It was driven, not by King Mogg, but by Queen Mogg.

'Well, we never thought of that,' said Adam. 'I suppose she's come up to start the decorating side. No – keep calm. They won't come near the stables. That's his side of the show. And when they've gone into the house, we can slip off.'

Queen Mogg had got stiffly out of her little car. She had a grey headscarf tied over her grey wispy hair. She was in the same drab dress in which she had confronted the children in the road outside Greens the previous week. Now she stood, peering up at the front of The Heron, her face even more furrowed and harassed than before, her hands still nervously rubbing together.

'One coat of paint'll have to do for the outside,' she began aggressively, while Mr. Wyborn was still only half-way up the drive. 'We can't possibly run to more. This place is already costing us far more than we'd anticipated. My brother's agreed to one coat . . .'

But Mr. Wyborn was also surveying the house from end to end. His lips pursed themselves until his fat face looked like a balloon.

'Lady,' Mr. Wyborn said, 'I've already given you my opinion. I've known this house for a great number of years. It's a fine house. They don't build like that these days. But it's in a shockin' state. Nothing bin done for years. Look at that woodwork – wicked! Now I give you an estimate the other day for makin' a nice job of it. One coat of paint – it'd be a false economy. We'd be back where we was after one winter. An' you an' the Major'd be blamin' me!'

'But there's the inside as well!' shrilled Miss Mogg. 'All the decorating – and damp patches on the first floor. If we give your firm the contract, they'll have to reduce the estimate.'

'Now the Major must've known this place needed money

spent on it when he took it. It went cheap in the market because it was going to cost a pretty penny to put right. It isn't no use him wastin' his money at this stage, makin' my firm do a half-job,' returned Mr. Wyborn inexorably.

Miss Mogg began visibly to panic. Perceiving victory on the horizon, Mr. Wyborn became magnanimous.

'Now, lady,' he said, 'my advice to you is to call in and see our managin' director. He'll meet you 'alf-way, I don't doubt. If you was to come in next Thursday afternoon between three and five – he's always there then –'

He'll have to estimate for those damp patches –'

'He'll do all of that,' said Mr. Wyborn firmly. 'Sounds to me like gutters. I'll have a look when we're inside. I can get at them from those winders . . .'

Mr. Wyborn, moving like a rolling ball, Miss Mogg half-running as if she were chasing it – together they disappeared into the house.

In the stable Sandra and Adam looked at each other.

'Good job we didn't follow the original idea, and take the spare key from the wall,' said Adam. 'She'd certainly have wondered how the gates came to be unlocked. We'd better wait in here a few minutes until we're sure they're going to stop inside.'

'She is odd-looking,' said Sandra, leaning back against a loose-box, and wishing she could stop her hands from shaking. 'She looks so hunted and worried. You feel she might begin screaming at any moment.'

'If I had Mogg for a brother, and Weary for a great-nephew, I'd have been screaming the house down years ago. And if you're beginning to feel sympathetic towards Queen Mogg, just remember how sickeningly mean she is, and how we had to go without our pie to provide her customers with what she should have given them. You'll be getting soft about Uncle Arthur next.'

'Oh, no, I won't,' said Sandra. 'And how are we going to get out of here? If we go back through the hole in the fence, she and Mr. Wyborn may be hanging out of the back windows, and if we go out through the gates, they may be hanging out of the front. I don't see how we're going to be able to tell. And, please, Adam, I'd like to go soon. I don't very much like being here.'

But Adam was occupying the delay with an inspection of the stables.

'They're in pretty good condition,' he said. 'He's had the repairs done in here. Look at the draining, and all that concrete. He does care about his horses, doesn't he?'

'There are those halters he had in the car this morning,' said Sandra. 'He was coming to The Heron.'

'There's a sack of some sort of feed down there, too,' said Adam. 'I wonder if he's proposing to bring a couple of his show-jumpers over. He couldn't, though, with nobody here to look after them. It's going to be a wonderful place, though, when he really gets it going. Eulalia says he's got a paddock just up the road for the jumps –'

'Adam,' said Sandra from by the half-door. 'There's someone else coming. It's not King Mogg, because he wouldn't be bobbing about outside the gates. Somebody's bobbing. I think two people are bobbing. And one of them's Julian –'

'And the other – oh, give me just one tiny guess – is Weary,' said Adam. 'They look from the way they're carrying on as if they've come on some sort of reconnoitre, like us. They can't see the Mogg car because it's round the curve. But they can't make out why the gates are open. Next time they take a peep, wave hard. But wave them *away*, or they'll think we mean them to join us, and they might be seen from the house.'

Just then, both heads reappeared. Sandra and Adam

simultaneously leaned over the half-door, making slow waving gestures that plainly said, 'Go away. Go away.'

Julian's head promptly withdrew. Weary took no notice. Slowly the whole of his small person appeared, as he crept round the gate-post.

'Somebody's going to get a big, big shock,' said Adam. Sandra and Adam watched while he tiptoed up the drive. Then – 'Surprise!' said Adam, as a look of horrified recognition spread over Weary's face when the Mogg car came into his line of vision. For a second he stood para- lysed. Then he scampered away out of sight.

'Serve him right!' and Adam. 'He'd probably been told to stay indoors. I must say he does ask for it. He must have seen great-auntie go belting off, and he never thought of her coming up here.'

Sandra was leaning again over the half-door. She was listening intently.

'I believe I heard a window open at the back of the place,' she said.

Adam listened.

'You did,' he said. 'There's another one. That just suits us. Because if we can go out through the gates, and not by the fence, we'll probably still find Julian outside.'

They took the chance, and ran swiftly and silently down the drive, out through the open gates, and into The Heron Ride. There – on the opposite side of the road, sitting quietly under a tree, shoulders hunched, arms hugging his knees – was Julian. When he saw them, he smiled, and rose to his feet.

'Weary's made off,' he said in low tones. 'You looked as if you were about to make a get-away, so I waited on the off-chance. I suppose it's Miss Mogg up there?'

'Come to have a nice argy-bargy with the decorator,' said Adam.

Julian looked at his watch.

'It probably won't be so very long before they all come back from the Downs. I made an excuse not to go with them, so I'd rather not be found hanging about here.'

'Come back with us,' said Adam. 'We're going down to the Mill Pool, and then home through the woods.'

Julian's face lit up. 'I'd heard there was a pool somewhere in these woods,' he said. 'But I've never come on it. I wanted to see it.'

Adam led the way. Sandra came next. Julian followed. It was a long slippery scramble down the precipitous slope. They went silently down between the trees, as if into a dark basin. At the bottom, except for one broad patch of sunlight, the pool lay still and black. The tree-tops alone were catching the late evening light.

Julian stood by the pool, his head raised, a listening expression upon his face.

'What do you hear?' said Adam, thinking Julian might already have heard the horses.

'A blackbird,' said Julian, his long face absorbed and pleased.

Sandra and Adam listened, too. A blackbird was singing his evening song high over their heads in the sunlit tree-tops above the quiet pool.

XI

'WHY did you come to The Heron?'

The three children had walked round the pool to have a look at the Mill itself, and now Adam put the question to Julian. They were standing in a line, surveying the rotting clapboard front.

'To see if there were bolts on the gates,' answered Julian, withdrawing his gaze from the rusted, twisted iron hoist still showing a fragment of dangling rope. 'Why did you?'

'To see if there were bolts on the gates,' said Adam. 'And there are.'

Julian had stepped forward to peer into the dank, dark interior. But the smell of decay and mouldering sacking on the floor was unpleasant. He turned back in the doorway to look out over the pool.

'I got worried – more worried even than I was in your garden this morning,' he said. 'The whole idea of a strike seemed somehow – so silly.'

'They all seem like a kindergarten on the loose,' said Adam tartly.

'And I could just see Major Mogg –'

'So could we!' said Sandra.

'Anyway, I let them all go off. I said I was taking my camera into the woods. And then I saw Miss Mogg start out. I was just beating it myself when Weary turned up, and said he'd show me exactly where the key was, so that I didn't have to waste time hunting.'

'We found a hole in the fence,' said Sandra.

'I never thought of that. Could Major Mogg get through it too?' said Julian.

'No – it's all right. It's too small –' said Adam.

'Even after all Adam's done to it,' said his sister.

'Oh,' said Julian with a sigh. 'They are silly.'

He stretched his arms with their long bony wrists up above his head, as if he were glad for a little while to be free of silly people.

'But you can't stop people who've got one idea in their heads,' he went on. 'I stopped trying in your garden this morning.'

They began to walk slowly and meditatively round the pool to where it narrowed to become part of the Long Meadow stream. It was so silent that instinctively they had lowered their voices, feeling that the sounds might carry too far across the water.

'Is it really as bad at Greens as Harry makes out?' asked Adam. 'Is there truly not enough to eat, and don't you really get any proper riding?'

'He does exaggerate a bit,' said Julian. 'But only a bit. Miss Mogg is terribly mean about food. We never seem to get enough to feel properly full. And as for the riding – something does seem to have gone completely wrong. I just can't make it out.'

'Sylvia kept saying that nobody took any interest in them,' said Sandra. 'We wondered if Mogg was bored with having taken over the tail-end of the Greens' kind of place, and wasn't going to take any trouble until he was able to start his own kind of crack school up at The Heron.'

'It's partly that, I think,' said Julian. 'My father, who knows him, said he hadn't particularly wanted to take over Greens. But he did want a nucleus of pupils to start his own school with, and so he agreed to take over the summer and autumn bookings. But I think he's been pretty

bored by it. And he's not the kind of man to stand being
bored. He's used to older pupils who really want to work
hard, and do him credit.'

They were now talking with such absorption that they
had automatically sat down by the edge of the pool.

'I remember my father saying that Major Mogg was a
fine soldier, but reckless and bad-tempered – and Heaven
help everybody if he wasn't kept occupied! He'd involve
himself in stupid things. Father said once he only avoided
court martial by the skin of his teeth. Then, when the war
hotted up, he went and got the M.C. I've been wondering,
actually, if something was going on now. Because I heard
Miss Mogg screaming at him the other day, "I know you've
got yourself into some sort of mischief. You always do.
You always have done, ever since you were a boy!" '

'Must be unnerving for her,' said Adam.

'She looks dreadfully ill with it,' said Julian. 'The whole
show must be awful for her.'

'If he's got himself tied up in something, it would
account for his mind not being on Sylvia and Eve,' said
Adam. 'Except they *must* bore him so. A man like that
who's had really good riders under him.'

'That school of his in the West Country was terrific,' said
Julian. 'My father said it was worth putting up with
Mogg's temper for what you got out of riding there. He
only sold it because he was getting older, and this new
venture at The Heron was to be smaller and more manage-
able. He may not like something smaller and more man-
ageable, even when he gets it going.'

'Are you keen on riding yourself?' asked Sandra.

Julian shook his head.

'No – not particularly. But my family is. My brothers
and sisters all hunt. My parents don't mind that I'd rather
do things like bird-watching. But they'd like me to be able

to ride decently. They wrote to Major Mogg, wanting me to go to his other school. But it was too late. He'd just sold it. I don't in the least mind being here. Only, as things are, it all seems a waste of time.'

'Harry's nearly in a frenzy about it being a waste of time,' said Adam.

They all laughed at the memory of poor Harry's frenzy.

'Harry does mind,' said Julian soberly. 'He's the only one – apart from Mogg – who really cares for horses. His father and brothers are all mad on car-racing. Harry's a throw-back to his great-grandfather. His grandfather turned his great-grandfather's stable of cab-horses into a garage, and his father turned that into a chain of garages. Harry'd like to turn it back to horses!'

'He misses the Greens themselves, too,' said Sandra.

'Well, it was like coming home for Harry,' said Julian. 'I don't think his stepmother really wants him in Brixton. And neither do Sylvia's and Eve's parents really want them tagged on. It was a bad day for everybody when the Greens packed it in. Sylvia and Eve don't really care about riding. They only do it because it's the O.K. thing to do in their neighbourhood. They'd all rather have a home like Greens than a crack riding school like The Heron.'

'All except Ethne. All she wants is to stick on a horse long enough to get out of range of the camera,' said Adam with a grin.

Julian frowned. 'It's odd about Ethne,' he began.

But just then a hullabaloo broke out high up in the direction of The Heron, the noise carrying with piercing clarity across the tranquil water.

'That's Queen Mogg screaming away,' said Sandra.

They sat, listening while the screeching continued. Every now and again they could hear a man's voice.

'That can't be King Mogg,' said Adam. 'We'd have heard the horses. Here –' he got up – 'something's happened. I'm going up to have a look.'

By the time Julian and Sandra saw Adam reach the top of the slope the noise had died down. They sat peacefully on by the pool. Suddenly a fish jumped near by.

'Oh,' said Sandra. 'What a pity Adam missed that fish! It would have encouraged him. He thinks there's an otter round this pool, and that it accounts for there being no fish down our part of the stream.'

'I wouldn't think that's because of an otter,' said Julian, with the same air of quiet authority that Onkel Anton had exhibited his first evening over the horses. 'It's something of a myth that otters scare off fish.' And then he asked: 'Do you fish, too ?'

'No,' said Sandra, 'I ride – Toby.' She went on seriously, 'The Horse is a Noble Animal, but you might not guess it from seeing Toby, although he is much better . . .'

Julian nodded. 'The Horse *is* a Noble Animal,' he said equally seriously. 'My father says people seem to forget it these days, and just push horses around. But why has Toby become better ?'

'Because,' said Sandra proudly, 'we have a groom from the Imperial Riding School in Vienna staying with us.'

Julian's face lit with his keen smile. 'The Lipizzaners,' he said. 'My father's been to Piber.'

'My mother went, too – years and years ago,' said Sandra eagerly.

And Julian began to tell her things about the Lipizzaners that his father had told him. Some of them she knew because Onkel Anton had told her, and some of them were new. She listened attentively to Julian's tales as the sun moved down the sky, and its light passed farther across the tree-tops.

T—E

When Julian had finished his store of Lipizzaner-knowledge, in return Sandra told him about the garden of The Heron. She told him about the heron itself, and how they had found the little lead replica standing in the middle of the lily leaves.

'Oh,' said Julian, 'I hope they don't mend the hole in the fence before I get a chance to get in, and see for myself.'

They had both forgotten Adam. There was a footstep behind them, and there he was, back with them.

'I've been talking to Queen Mogg,' he announced with triumph.

'Did she catch you snooping?' asked Sandra anxiously.

Adam looked offended.

'There wasn't any question of "snooping", as you call it. I went straight up the drive, and I could see her standing by the car, haranguing Mr. Wyborn. And I realized I didn't have to pretend. I simply said we'd been swimming down in the pool, and we'd heard a racket. And I'd come up to see. And what do you think had happened?'

'Well, what?' said Sandra, who had become more interested in Julian's stories of the Lipizzaners, and her own about the heron.

'She and Mr. Wyborn had come out of the house, and they'd got into the car, and the moment they started to back, whe-ew – the near tyre went flat! And when they looked – there was a whacking great nail in it! She was carrying on about somebody having crept up the drive, and put it there on purpose.'

'She's got a hateful, suspicious mind,' said Sandra.

'Well, I wonder,' said Adam, exchanging a meaningful glance with Julian.

'Weary does keep nails in his pocket,' murmured Julian. They started off through the wood, which was darker than Sandra and Adam had yet seen it. Once they pulled up to have a rest under the big oak tree, and once they stopped, still as sentinels, when Julian pointed silently to a tiny stoat, creeping home across a clearing, a wicked expression on its wedge-like face for the fright they were giving it.

When they were about to come out under the open sky of the fields, Adam remembered something. 'What were you going to say about Ethne?' he asked Julian. 'You began to say something was odd.'

'Only that I just don't know what's in Ethne's mind. When we left your garden this morning, she started to bubble and giggle with excitement as if she'd been holding back some secret. And she giggled and skipped and was maddening all the way back. And then, at Greens, she took the others into a corner, and they started off, too. But they weren't going to tell me. It was something to do with their strike.'

'Sounds most sinisterly to me,' said Adam, 'as if our Baby Starlet had managed to think up – did I say *think* up – some improvement on Harry's original scheme.'

'That's what I thought,' said Julian placidly. 'And since I'm not going to be counted in anyway, I'm not going to be told what it is.'

'Still,' said Sandra, stopping to shake dried earth from her sandal, 'still, of all of them – somehow – Ethne does *work*.'

'Come hell or flood, she does,' assented Adam.

'She jolly well *means* to stick on a horse,' said Julian. 'Nothing really interests Ethne –'

'– but Ethne's career,' finished Adam.

But Julian had raised an imperative hand.

'Listen.'

Far away, muffled by the woods behind them, they

could hear up the hill, beyond the stream, the distant sounds of horses' hooves.

'That'll be them going home,' said Julian.

By the time they had crossed the second field, and threaded their way through the spinney, and then turned sharply up Long Meadow, it was later than Sandra and Adam usually returned home. The sky was turning a darker blue, promising nightfall, and the cows were already out of the meadow. They could be seen quietly making their way across the Glebe, in front of the boy with the stick.

'You don't need the ticking of your watch here,' said Adam. 'You measure the time by the cows coming and going.'

They came in a leisurely way up to Miss Vaughan's white gate. There, waiting for them in the garden, were Miss Vaughan and Onkel Anton. Since the sun was off the plants, Miss Vaughan had been watering, and Onkel Anton had been gallantly carrying her little watering-can. Each snapdragon had a minute, perfect, dark wet circle of earth round its base.

'This is Julian,' said Sandra. 'He was here this morning with the others, but I don't expect you really looked at him. His father has been to Piber, and has told him all about the Lipizzaners.'

Miss Vaughan smiled at Julian, and Onkel Anton stepped forward to shake hands.

'You are then a keen rider?' he said kindly to Julian.

'No – not very,' said Julian simply. 'I'm a bird-watcher – though I do love horses. But I don't know as much about them as I do about birds.'

'Each man to his last,' said Miss Vaughan.

They all five walked up the garden, and through the cool, dim cottage to the front door. Julian said goodbye, and they stood in a cluster at the door to wave to him as he went down the path and turned into the lane to make his way back through the village to Greens.

The evening was particularly pleasant. After supper, Miss Vaughan, Onkel Anton, and the two children sat out under the apple trees, watching the dusk go, and the night come, and the moon rise beyond the Downs. They heard the nightingale singing in the spinney by the stream, and they heard Toby give a great piercing neigh from somewhere in the Glebe, answering the nightingale. Onkel Anton and Miss Vaughan talked about Vienna and the lives that they had lived there. It was talk about the past, but it was happy talk, because they had been happy people. The world of Mogg and Uncle Arthur seemed a long way off.

Later, Sandra dropped into Adam's attic room. She found him kneeling on the window-seat, staring out into the garden. The moon was higher, and beginning to flood the garden with a silver light. So bright was it that almost every beech tree at the bottom of Long Meadow could be seen.

Sandra sat down upon the window-seat. 'I like Julian,' she said. 'I like every one of them – even if they are often dreadfully silly. But I like Julian the most. And I would like to visit his home in the country, and meet his brothers and sisters, and his mother, and his father, who says The Horse *is* a Noble –'

'So did I like him,' said Adam. 'Look – there's the Great Bear – and those stars there are Cassiopeia – and there's Aldebaran –'

'Are you *sure*?' said Sandra doubtfully, peeping out at the great sea of stars sweeping over Long Meadow Cottage.

'No. I am not at *all* sure,' said Adam, with dignity. 'I shall ask Eulalia in the morning.'

'He's going to have a difficult time at Greens if they're going to leave him out of things,' said Sandra. 'I'd like to know what Ethne thinks she's up to. We ought to know, now that we've got ourselves so involved in it all.'

'Who's involved?' said Adam, withdrawing his head from contemplation of the heavens.

'Why, us, of course,' said Sandra, surprised.

'No, we aren't. We've had a busy day of it – what with you giving them our lunch this morning, and us going to The Heron this afternoon, and hearing about the strike scheme. But that'll finish it. We probably won't see any of them again. Why should we? We haven't got any plans to meet them. And nobody's suggested that we should.'

'You mean – we aren't involved?'

'Not in the least.'

The two children stared gloomily at each other as the moonlight began to steal into the attic.

XII

THE next morning Sandra awoke to the stuttering call of a
left-over cuckoo, as it fled across the stream at the bottom
of Long Meadow. She dressed in the sunlight streaking the
floor-boards by the window, singing an old folk-song called
'Oh, the Cuckoo, She's a Pretty Bird'.

At the second verse, a diversion occurred. The telephone began to ring in the hall. She opened her door at the
same instant that Adam opened his. Both raced downstairs together. Adam arrived first.

Hanging over the banisters, Sandra watched him pick up
the receiver. After a moment, she saw his face change to
that of an elderly family solicitor, but happily not to
Uncle Arthur's. 'Oh dear,' he kept saying pompously, and
then in shocked tones, 'Tut.' Finally, with great self-im-
portance, he said, 'I shall tell Miss Vaughan at once – at
once. We will communicate with you immediately we
receive news.'

Tut-tutting to himself and taking no notice of Sandra,
he put the receiver down with an abstracted air. Then,
excitement triumphing, he tore into the kitchen where
Miss Vaughan – who had not heard the telephone – was
lifting the bread out of the bread bin.

'Whaddya know!' Adam threw his arms round his
Eulalia, and spun her round, loaf and all. 'It's Paul! The
Little Refugee Child! He's run away! That was the family
he'd gone to in York by mistake. Oh, you were quite right.
He couldn't have liked them. She sounded one of those
mincey-wincey females, and she kept saying, "Tell Miss

Whosit it reely wasn't our fault. We'd only asked him to help with the baby." '

'Ach,' said Onkel Anton crossly. He had come into the kitchen behind Sandra in time to hear the excitement. 'Many times it is the same story. A poor refugee is invited into the home for a holiday, and there he finds he is invited to replace the servant one no longer has. It is not he who is to have the holiday! They have learned their lesson, these people. Now Paul is gone. I am not surprised. You will see. He will come here. Tonight he will arrive.'

'But there's you,' wailed Sandra. 'What about you? Oh, you won't have to go and look after the mincey-wincey female's baby, will you?'

Onkel Anton spread his hands out with the same desolate gesture as on his first evening. He rolled his eyes expressively. Consternation fell visibly upon Adam as well as Sandra.

'No, of course Onkel Anton's not going off to baby-sit, and he knows it,' said Miss Vaughan with brisk common sense. 'We can't possibly part with him. He's become one of the family. Paul will sleep in Onkel Anton's room — which was the original plan, after all — and Onkel Anton will sleep at the Vicarage. I foresaw this situation, and I had a word with the Vicar, who is delighted at the bare idea.'

'Suppose Paul's lost our address?' said Sandra, wreathed in smiles at Onkel Anton's reprieve.

'That,' admitted Miss Vaughan, 'is a much greater worry.'

All eyes turned to Onkel Anton.

'Paul is a most capable boy,' said Onkel Anton, a shade doubtfully.

'I shall not myself,' said Miss Vaughan, 'feel entirely

happy until I actually see Paul with my own eyes safely housed in Long Meadow Cottage!'

With all this excitement, speculations about Greens were in abeyance for about an hour and a half. Sandra and Adam were sprawling with books under the shade of the apple trees. In the far distance, beyond the Glebe, the portly form of Toby could be seen plodding up and down the Vicar's lawn in front of the antiquated mower, guided by the old man who gardened twice a week at the Vicarage.

'Work Day, Work Day,' sang Adam, like a telly commercial.

'Which do you think Toby prefers?' said Sandra.

'You or the mower?' said Adam. 'I should think he's deeply thankful to be back with the mower. He doesn't have to use his brain there.'

'You know –' Sandra changed the subject – 'we don't have to go on guessing when Harry will stage his silly strike. We know.'

'No, we don't. Even Julian didn't know. They won't tell him anything.'

'We knew before Harry did,' said Sandra.

'What on earth do you mean?'

'Well, think,' said Sandra. 'They've got to find a time when *both* Moggs are out of the way. We agreed on that. They won't bother about that old groom. I heard Harry say King Mogg was sacking him anyway, so he won't care what they do. But Miss Mogg would screech the place down.'

'Harry'll certainly have got around to that problem by now,' said Adam. 'But when isn't she there?'

'She isn't going to be there tomorrow afternoon,' said Sandra.

'How ever do you know that?'

'Because it's Thursday. We heard Mr. Wyborn telling

her to go and see the managing director of his firm in Ardsham between three and five. I'm certain they'll seize the
chance. After all, what preparations have they got to
make ? All they've got to do is to saddle the horses and go.
They *know* King Mogg is always over at his friend's place
in the early part of the afternoon.'

'Well, there's nothing we can do about it. If we're about
here, we may see them go up The Heron Ride. And I suppose we may hear later what happened, if we run into any
of them in the village. Otherwise –' he sat up and looked
about him – 'otherwise, we may never hear anything
about the strike at all. Goodness, it's hotter than ever today. I wouldn't be surprised if we didn't get a thunderstorm
out of all this. The heat-wave can't go on much longer.'

All through the afternoon it seemed to get hotter. The
children went down to the stream and found it even more
shrunk than yesterday. All the cows were standing in the
water, and eyed Sandra and Adam reproachfully as if
blaming them for the torrid day. The brown grass in the
meadow seemed to crackle underfoot with heat. The sky
overhead was almost white.

'There'll be a storm,' prophesied Adam.

And that evening Sandra, who had returned to the
stream to collect a book she had left beneath the beech
trees, reported that she had seen a pair of swallows skim-
ming low along the water. 'They always fly low when
there's rain coming,' she said.

But no rain fell that day. Only in the night Sandra was
woken by the low, menacing, distant growl of thunder
somewhere beyond the Downs. Before she dropped asleep,
lightning had flickered up and down the walls. And once
she heard the rise and fall of a sudden wind among the
trees. But no storm came.

For the first time since she and Adam had arrived at

Long Meadow, the early morning was grey and the clouds louring as if the sky could not much longer keep back the rain. When she put her head out of the bedroom window, the air seemed even more stifling than yesterday, and very still – not with the tranquil stillness of other summer mornings, but as if some badness in the weather lay in hiding just beyond the woods.

It was the first time that breakfast was indoors. When she came downstairs, she found Onkel Anton and Miss Vaughan already in the dining-room. Miss Vaughan was looking perturbed.

'I sat up quite late last night,' she was saying to Onkel Anton. 'I had a feeling that he might easily walk in after the last train.'

'It is possible that he has lost the address,' admitted Onkel Anton. 'But I beg that you do not disturb yourself. If you, Madame, had seen as much as I of these children, you would not be disturbed. Paul is a careless boy. But irresponsible – no! And a boy who – with others older, it is true – can find his way from Budapest to Austria, who can make for himself a passage through barbed wire at the frontier – that one, I do not think will easily be at a loss between York and Long Meadow Cottage.'

Onkel Anton applied himself placidly to his boiled egg. Miss Vaughan remained only partially convinced. After breakfast she telephoned the station and the post office to ascertain that there was no Hungarian boy awaiting collection at the one, or telegram awaiting delivery at the other.

'If Paul does not arrive before lunch,' she said with decision to Onkel Anton, 'I think that perhaps you and I will go into Ardsham and call at the police station. There will be no harm in your giving a description of him in case he has run out of money for fares, or – as appears most likely – lost our address.'

She was answered by a prolonged rumble of thunder many miles away.

Throughout the morning the children hung restlessly about. It was difficult to settle to any activity when they were speculating about Paul. At mid-morning they went down to the stream. But the water was an ugly leaden colour, and it was stifling under the beech trees. The Downs were standing out against the heavy sky, as though they were in the next field. The Heron seemed as sharply defined as if constructed of pewter, the trees about it a black, motionless phalanx. The children walked to the edge of the wood. It looked uninviting. They turned aimlessly back.

By lunch time there was still neither sign of Paul, nor message. Miss Vaughan took the bus time-table out of the drawer in the hall table.

After they washed up, Miss Vaughan and Onkel Anton – both providently carrying their macintoshes – left to catch the bus in the village. Adam accompanied them to the bus-stop. He returned to report to Sandra that Miss Mogg had swept past down the Ardsham road in the small car that she had taken up to The Heron that other afternoon.

'So you were right,' he said. 'And if it weren't for the weather, they probably would have chosen this afternoon for their idiotic performance.'

'I wonder if the weather really will stop them,' said Sandra. But somehow she no longer felt so interested in the affairs of Greens. Harry's exploits seemed to belong to the now-vanished heat-wave. She had become infected with the general anxiety about their Little Refugee Child, and was wishing that she had gone into Ardsham with Miss Vaughan and Onkel Anton.

The cottage seemed remarkably empty without either

Miss Vaughan or Onkel Anton. The children adjourned
to the long whitewashed playroom that Miss Vaughan had
added to the cottage for just such dreary and aimless
occasions. The walls were festooned with the long rolls
of brass-rubbings. Adam took them down, and spread
them out on the ping-pong table. Sandra sat at his side,
methodically cataloguing in an exercise-book what Adam
had scribbled down on the spot in his pocket notebook.

They worked quietly together for about half an hour.
It was when they were bending over the blackened, austere
rubbing of a knight gazing remotely up at the playroom
ceiling, that Sandra suddenly realized that she could not
see the detail because the room had become so dark. She
raised her head, and looked out through the window.

'Good gracious!' she began – and at that moment, there
came a flicker in the playroom – the merest twitch of light
– followed by a crashing peal of thunder immediately
above the Long Meadow chimney-pots. Then, on a rising,
swirling gust of wind, came the rain, slamming and beating against the windows and walls, while the lightning
raced up and down the sky. For the next half-hour it was
impossible to see beyond the white fence, though Sandra –
drawn with the excitement of the storm to the window –
once saw the wind sweep back the curtain of rain to reveal
the beeches tossing at the bottom of the meadow, and
beyond the beeches the black Downs, and, outlined as if
by a steel pen against the woods, The Heron.

Unmoved by the storm, Adam still bent over his brass-
rubbings. Sandra finally returned to his side. Apart from
the storm, the room was silent.

Suddenly there was another blinding flash, followed by
an artillery roll of thunder around the sky.

'What's that?' said Sandra.

Adam had also looked up. It seemed unlikely in all the

din and clatter that they should be hearing – but there it
was again! A small, insistent tap-tap – tap-tap – at the
window! There pressed against the streaming glass – was
a small white face under a macintosh hood.

'It's Weary!' said Sandra. 'It's Weary!'

She dashed to the door.

In a rush of gale, Weary was blown into the playroom,
dripping and shining with rain. He stood wordless, in the
middle of the floor, while Sandra efficiently peeled off his
hood and his macintosh. Already little puddles of water
were collecting round his feet.

Adam had got up from the table, and come across the
room. Together, he and Sandra stood looking down at
Weary, while he thwacked his arms round his skinny little
body, and stamped his feet.

'What's happened?' said Sandra. 'Weary, what's happened?'

Weary continued to stamp and thwack. He said nothing.

'Where are the others?' said Adam.

'Gone,' said Weary. 'Everybody's gone.'

Gone – and left Weary alone in the house with the
frightening storm coming over the Downs at him! No
wonder, thought Sandra compassionately, the little boy
had become terrified, and run out into the rain and the
thunder and the wind to find his friends at Long Meadow.

But Adam's mind was on other things.

'Not Harry and the others gone!' he exclaimed. 'You
don't mean they've taken the horses through the storm to
The Heron!'

But Weary shook his head vigorously.

'They went long before it started,' he said, rocking himself to and fro. 'Me grandfather went off. Me great-auntie –
she went off. And Harry – he said, "Now we can go!"
An' Sylvia says, "There's thunder coming." An' Harry says,

"If we go now, we'll beat the thunder." An' they went. They went.'

He began humming his airy-fairy tuneless little tune. Sandra looked narrowly at him, as he wagged his head and jogged about. She remembered that little tune – and how Weary had hummed it that morning in the lane with Toby and Onkel Anton when he had been trying to tell them how frightened he had been of the scene between his grandfather and Harry. She began to wonder if Weary always hummed to himself when he was frightened, and must be left to tell his story in his own way. Could there be anything now that had frightened Weary – beyond an empty house, and a thunderstorm ?

'Where's Julian ?' Adam was asking.

'Gone,' said Weary. 'Before the others. He went up into the woods.'

Weary's eyes were now roving about the playroom. More than ever, Sandra was convinced that he was terrified of something beyond the storm. He had come to tell them his terror. But to find Weary's terror needed as much patience as exploring a maze.

Adam had turned back to his brass-rubbings. It seemed to Sandra as if he had all at once become bored with Weary, and the goings-on of Harry and his friends.

Then, without raising his head from his contemplation of the austere knight, Adam said, 'I expect the others were pleased when they realized they were all alone in the house. And that there was nobody to stop them going to The Heron. Nobody at all.'

And Sandra guessed, from Adam's casual manner, that he knew there was a maze to be explored – that Weary had some further tale to tell.

'Yes,' said Weary. 'Nobody to stop them.'

He began to wander round the playroom, humming

lightly and balancing the ping-pong rackets on the back of his hand.

'Me grandfather can't stop them,' he informed the children.

'He's gone, I suppose, to watch his show-jumpers?' prompted Sandra.

'Mmm,' nodded Weary.

There was another long silence. A more feeble burst of rain spattered the windows. But the thunder seemed to be farther away. It looked as if the storm might be moving off.

'Heard him talkin' to me great-auntie,' said Weary. 'Said he wasn't coming home. Said he was goin' straight to The Heron.'

'Straight to The Heron!' exclaimed Sandra and Adam together.

'But doesn't he always come back to Greens first, to collect everyone up for the evening ride?' asked Adam quickly.

'Isn't goin' to be no evening ride,' said Weary detachedly.

He stole a sidelong glance at Sandra. Then he eyed Adam who, apparently totally unconcerned, had returned once more to his brass-rubbings.

'*He* wuz in the passage. *She* started off at him. *He* shouted. *She* cried – me great-auntie cried. She said, "You're runnin' into trouble. What you goin' do this afternoon? I know you're up to somethin'. Nothin' don't change you," she said. An' he pushed her away, and she fell against the wall, an' he shouted – he shouted –'

'What did he shout?' said Sandra.

' "*There isn't goin' to be trouble, you ole fool*" – an' he went to the cupboard in the passage – an' – an' –'

The storm had not gone. There was a blinding flash, and a crash of thunder that shook the playroom.

'He shouted, "*I gotta gun. How can there be trouble when I gotta gun?*"' screamed Weary – and hurled himself upon Sandra, burying his face in her sheltering arms.

But Adam had left his brass-rubbings. He came over to Sandra and Weary. Firmly he took the little boy from Sandra, and turned him gently so that Weary was looking up into his eyes.

'Your grandfather – Major Mogg – was taking a gun?' he asked quietly. 'He was going up to The Heron with a *gun?*'

XIII

'Was it an air-gun? Was it a rook-rifle?'

Weary shook his head.

'Are you quite sure?' pursued Adam. 'You know what they look like, do you, Weary? Because your grandfather could very easily be going out into the fields round The Heron to shoot birds. That's nothing. Most of the farmers round here shoot birds, you know.'

But Weary was shaking his head with determination.

'I saw the little gun,' he whispered.

'Where were you?' asked Sandra.

'I wuz peepin' through the banisters, an' I saw me grandfather gettin' angry – and he *got* angry, an' he went to the cupboard in the hall, an' he pushed the door open wide, and he put his hand up to the little shelf I can't reach, an' he took it out, an' he shouted, "There!" An' me great-auntie screamed an' she said, "Oh, you oughta have handed that in when you come out of the Army. All these years – I knew it wuz lyin' round somewhere. You brought it with you here –" '

'What did your grandfather say?' asked Adam.

'He said, "You've always interfered, and the other three'd be carryin' guns –" '

'*The other three?*' exclaimed Adam.

The cottage seemed deathly silent. In the distance the thunder was still faintly rumbling. But the wind had dropped. The rain had stopped. The only sound was the steady drip-drip from the apple trees outside.

From the expression on Adam's face, Sandra could see that he was thinking fast.

'You're sure you heard your grandfather say he was going straight to The Heron before returning home?'

Weary nodded.

Adam turned to Sandra.

'We'll have to warn Harry up at The Heron,' he said. 'They'll have to pack it in. Mogg – and three others – all with guns. They're going up to The Heron on some game of their own. It was just stupid before – that strike business. Now it's gone dangerous. Either they'll have to bring the horses straight back down The Heron Ride to Greens. Or they'll have to leave the horses in the stables up there – they'll be perfectly all right with Mogg coming – and come back this way along the stream. *But they must – they just must – get out.*'

'You mean,' said Sandra, with sinking heart, 'we'll have to go up to The Heron to tell them –'

'Not "we". One of us,' said Adam. 'The other's got to go into Ardsham, and find Eulalia and Onkel Anton – or if no Eulalia and Onkel Anton – then straight to the police station. But with any luck, they'll still be busy describing Paul in the police station. I hope he's difficult to describe, and that Onkel Anton's accent is hard to understand, and that it all takes ages. Actually we could telephone the police right away, but I'd much rather we got hold of Eulalia before bringing them into it – even if we can only breathe a word down her ear while she's telling them about Paul.'

'But it's not bad enough to get the police in!' protested Sandra, shocked.

'Yes, it is,' said Adam. 'Because I think Julian was right, and that something is going on. You don't have four people converging on an empty, isolated house carrying Service revolvers for a joke. But I'd much rather find Eulalia and Onkel Anton, because they really will know what ought to be done. The main thing, though, is to get Harry and the others out of The Heron. It's going to be no moment for King Mogg and his friends to turn up, thinking the place is empty, and find Harry playing the fool and trying to keep them out – not if they've really got guns.'

'I wish we could get at Julian,' said Sandra dismally.

'Well, we can't,' returned Adam. 'Which would you rather do? Which, as they say, is most *you*? Thumb a lift, with Weary, into Ardsham? You'd be there in ten minutes. Or go up to The Heron, and somehow persuade those idiots to clear out?'

'You go to Ardsham,' said Sandra, feeling sick with dismay. 'The police'll listen to you. I'll go along the stream to The Heron.'

'You can't,' said Adam. 'Think of what that mud'll be like after this downpour!'

'But there isn't *time* to walk up The Heron Ride,' began Sandra, and stopped. 'Oh, I know,' she said. 'I'll take Toby. I saw him just now out in the Glebe. He'd found himself a sheltered spot against the hedge.'

Adam was peering through the windows.

'The storm's gone off,' he said. 'It may come back, but it's all right now. I don't like you taking Toby out in a storm, but I think it's the best thing.'

Sandra was buttoning Weary back into his macintosh. She got her own and Adam's down from the pegs at the end of the playroom – macintoshes and Wellington boots.

'Will you ever manage to get a lift to Ardsham?' she asked.

'Yes,' said Adam briefly.

And Sandra knew that he would.

They parted outside the cottage, Adam and Weary going off down the front path, Sandra tramping over the soaking, squelching Long Meadow turf to the Glebe gate.

In the Glebe she found that Toby had returned to his usual stance in mid-meadow. He did not appear to be unduly wet, or perturbed by the storm. Sandra guessed that he was pretty tough over bad weather. She had called in at the shed to collect saddle and bridle. There was a bad moment when Toby coldly surveyed her ingratiating approach, and made to move off down the Glebe. Then he decided to behave graciously, and allowed her to heave the bridle over his damp, tousled ears, and refrained from his favourite joke of blowing himself out and then collapsing when she was struggling with the girths.

At last she led him through the Glebe gate, back across Long Meadow, and through the gate in the Long Meadow hedge into The Heron Ride. There, apprehensively, she mounted him. Soberly, Toby moved off up The Heron Ride.

For the first hundred yards Toby walked decorously as though in a procession. Suddenly fearful that King Mogg might come tootling past early on his way up to The Heron, Sandra boldly touched Toby's flanks with her heels. Wet tarmac and all, Toby broke into – for him – a smart trot. Sandra drew a nervous breath, and sat down to it. For a girl who aimed at a Lipizzaner, she was doing fine. Across her memory flicked her cry to Adam – was it really only the other day? – *'I'm never going to look right on a horse.'* In a crumpled plastic mac and Wellingtons, she could hardly be looking 'right' – 'but,' said Sandra spiritedly, 'what do I care!'

She paid immediately for her bravado because it communicated itself to Toby, who instantly entered into the spirit of the thing by bursting into a rollicking canter. Together they rocked perilously up The Heron Ride.

The stream, as they crossed it, was already swollen and rushing. When the road began its uphill climb, the trees closed round it. Through the tree-trunks, blackened by rain, Sandra caught glimpses of the Downs, sullen against a sky that seemed once more to be darkening. As Toby slowed his pace against the steepening gradient, she saw a ragged fork of lightning streak impatiently down the clouds. A low rumble over the horizon confirmed her suspicions. The storm was threatening to return.

'There is not,' said Sandra to herself, 'going to be any choice between bringing the horses back down The Heron Ride, and leaving them in the stables.' They would have to be left in the stables – and Toby would have to be left with them, while she took the others down to shelter in the old Mill. She hoped King Mogg would hardly notice Toby's presence among the Greens horses. She hoped the Vicar would not mind his odd-job pony being involved in the whole affair!

At last the road wound itself up to the point where she and Onkel Anton and Weary had encountered King Mogg and his car. There was the signpost in the hedge. There was the telephone kiosk from which Harry was going to telephone King Mogg to say they'd withdrawn labour to The Heron. And, down the lane to the left, she could see the wet, gleaming roofs of the cottages that made up the tiny hamlet near the Mill. The sight of those roofs was comforting after the long, lonely corkscrew ride up from Long Meadow through the woods. For it meant that there were people near, and not just trees!

Then she and Toby were past the hamlet, and again among the trees. The road gave some more corkscrew turns, and straightened out on to the level. Sandra gave a sigh of relief. There ahead of her lay the long, familiar, ancient wall of The Heron! She was there! Now – provided everybody was ready to listen to her – everything should be straightforward.

And there were the great double gates! As Toby drew level, Sandra noticed that the large padlock was swinging loose, unlocked. Somebody, then, really had taken the key. Somebody really was inside the gates.

She managed to draw Toby up opposite the padlock. She wheeled him to face the Heron gates. Then, in the silence that fell when Toby's clattering little hooves had stopped, she put her hand up to her mouth, and threw back her head to make her voice carry:

'Hi – i – i –' she called, her cry echoing into the cavern of the woods beyond The Heron. 'Hi – i – i – Har – ry!'

Like the call of a hunting-horn, the cry seemed to carry far up into and across the tree-tops. By way of answer, came a flurry of bird-movements among the foliage. And, by way of another answer, came the sinister grumble of the thunder prowling up on the Downs. But from inside

The Heron came no sound. It might have been a dead house.

'Har–ry!'

They must be there! Inside the stables! Down the garden, even! Sandra tried again, throwing her voice even farther across the silent woods:

'Har–ry. It's me! Sandra!'

No answer. Only another stirring of the birds in the trees, the dripping of the raindrops from the myriad leaves – and again the approaching mutter of the returning storm.

'I've got something to tell you! Please – please answer! It's terribly urgent!'

Suddenly, from immediately behind the gates, as if she had been hiding right up against them, came Ethne's cheery, important little voice:

'We're ever so busy, you know. We aren't letting anyone in.'

In Sandra exasperation mingled with relief:

'Ethne – it's serious! You must get out – all of you. Go and tell Harry. Major Mogg's coming straight here –'

'Oooh,' interrupted Ethne excitedly. 'Are you *sure*? Cos we haven't phoned him yet. It's too early for him to be back.'

'Who said Mogg was coming?'

Ethne had been joined by Harry. Sandra guessed that she had been left on guard inside the gate, while the others were in the stables, tying up the horses. The silence that she had found overhanging The Heron must have fallen only when they had heard Toby's hooves upon the road.

'Yes – who said so? Who said Mogg was coming?'

Sylvia, truculent, had joined Harry and Ethne.

'Somebody's making it up. Somebody wants to stop us from striking. But we aren't going to. So there!'

That was Eve! Sandra's heart sank. They were going to be silly and difficult after all.

'I'm not making it up,' she cried desperately. 'I've ridden all the way up from Long Meadow specially to tell you. He's got a gun. He's bringing three friends. They've got guns. No – no – it's nothing to do with you and your strike. It's something else. We don't know what. *But you must get out.*'

Something in Sandra's voice had struck home.

'You pulling our legs?'

For the first time a note of doubt sounded. It was Sylvia.

Then – 'Blackleg!' shouted Harry furiously. 'Blackleg! There's always those trying to undermine strikers! Clear off!'

' 'Sides,' came Ethne's wail, 'we can't go. It's too late. Sylvia, *remember you-know-what!*'

Sandra groaned with impatience. Just as Sylvia had been wavering, too! Why couldn't they go? Why was it too late? What was Ethne up to?

In her urgency Sandra was barely aware of the darkness gathering in the woods round her. She braced herself for one last effort.

'Harry,' she called. 'Sylvia – Eve – *listen –*'

But her words were drowned by the sudden swift rustling of all the leaves in the woods, as the rain poured down through them, and from round and around the sky came the crashing of the thunder.

Beaten and blinded by rain, Toby shook his head, and shook it again. For the first time he became visibly perturbed.

'Harry,' cried Sandra in panic. 'Let me in. Let me inside. I can't stay out in this –'

But all she heard through the roar of the storm was their

feet running, running up the gravel drive as they dived for the shelter of the stables.

'Harry –' she called, 'Harry – *please* –'

'It's all right, Sandra,' shouted a voice from inside the gates. 'Hang on – one second.'

It was a voice that she knew. But it was not one of their voices. She could not place it. But no matter. For behind the gates, somebody was drawing the great bolts. The left-hand gate was opening. Somebody was slowly swinging it back.

Toby waited for no invitation. As soon as there was enough opening, he marched through into the Heron drive. And instantly the gate was pushed to behind him and Sandra, the bolts rammed firmly home by Julian – Julian who, with the rain streaming down his face, seized Toby's bridle and led him to the stables, as the thunder roared over The Heron.

As Julian helped Sandra slide thankfully off Toby, the others closed angrily round him.

'Where did you come from?' shouted Harry.

'How did you get in?' shouted Sylvia.

By way of answer, Julian said nothing. He reminded Sandra of Onkel Anton dealing with King Mogg, when – in his own time – he replied coolly:

'I came up through the garden. I got into the garden by way of a hole in the fence. There was something I had been told about that I wanted to see in the garden. And while I was in the garden looking at it, I heard Sandra calling and calling.'

The silence was uncomfortable. Except for Ethne's twitter, like an upset blue-tit, nobody spoke. Eve traced a pattern on the concrete floor with the toe of her jodhpur boot.

Julian turned to Sandra.

'I heard you say Mogg was carrying a gun.'

'Weary came to tell Adam and me,' said Sandra exhaustedly. 'Adam's gone to Ardsham to tell the police.'

Julian wasted no further time. He turned back to the others.

'This isn't any moment for fooling,' he said. 'Something's happening. We can find out what later. It may turn out to be nothing at all. In the meantime, we'll have to clear out.'

Harry began to bluster, Ethne chirruping at his elbow. But Eve and Sylvia, for the first time, looked undecided. They exchanged glances. Eve nodded at Sylvia. Sylvia shrugged.

'O.K.,' she said. 'O.K., Julian.'

'Uh-huh,' echoed Eve.

There was a disbelieving howl from Harry.

'You can't all be gonna –'

But they could. The leadership had passed from Harry to Julian.

'Tie up Toby, Sandra,' said Julian.

The rain was slamming down upon the stable roof. The thunder rolled from end to end of the sky.

Julian's eyes passed along the line of stalls. Toby had quietened the moment he was allowed inside the gates. The Greens horses were all standing peacefully – all except Penny. As the lightning touched the stable walls, and the thunder flung itself across the roof-top, Penny pawed the ground infinitesimally with her near foreleg. Julian's eyes rested upon her. He opened his mouth to say something to Harry, but Harry had suddenly stiffened.

'There's a car coming,' he said.

Above the din and clatter of the storm, they could all hear what Harry had heard. But it was not a car. . . .

'It's much heavier than a car,' said Julian, leaning over the half-door to listen.

They were now all crowding behind Julian, drawing close behind his shoulders, as if he could protect them.

'It sounds more like a lorry. Or a heavy van,' said Julian. 'Everybody keep very quiet. It's stopping outside the gates.'

And then, very very slowly, it came to a standstill, across the top of the gates, towering over them.

'It looks like a furniture van,' whispered Sandra.

XIV

THE children saw the top of the furniture van draw to a lurching stop. Huddled inside the half-door of the stable, they waited in silence. And nothing happened – nothing except for a further gusty rising of wind in the woods round The Heron, a prolonged flash of lightning that lit their frightened faces, and another long-drawn-out roll of thunder.

'They've left the van, and gone away,' whispered Eve at last.

'I think they've noticed that the padlock is undone and they're discussing it among themselves,' said Julian.

Just then the gates shuddered, as somebody vigorously shoved from outside.

'We'll have to go – *now*,' said Julian under his breath. 'And we'll have to go the way I came in – through Sandra and Adam's hole in the fence. It's down towards the bottom of the garden. You go up the drive –'

But the rest of Julian's hurried instructions were lost in another roar of thunder.

And this time, from behind the children, came a responsive movement from one of the stalls. Harry looked quickly over his shoulder. Penny was now openly disliking the storm. Her ears were back, and one hoof was uneasily pawing at the concrete.

But nobody was interested in Penny. And nobody noticed that Harry left the group. All eyes were fastened upon the great double gates. Somebody outside was furiously shaking them.

'It's all right,' murmured Julian comfortingly. 'They won't break those bolts. But we'd better make a move. Because if Mogg and his friends mean to get into The Heron, sooner or later they'll do it. One by one – Sylvia first – and very quietly up the gravel, or they'll hear it crunch.'

'Where's Harry ?' said Sylvia.

Agitated, but carefully controlled, Harry's voice came from Penny's stall.

'Can't leave Penny,' he said. 'She'll hurt herself if she starts kicking.'

Standing by Penny's head, he murmured to her again, and stroked her nose. Reassured by Harry, Penny's ears had gone forward. She was standing still.

There was another flash of lightning that raked the stable, another crash of thunder, and then:

'What are they up to ?' said Eve in sudden terror.

For the engine of the furniture van was roaring. Over the gates the children saw the top of the van begin to shake, and then to recede slowly.

'They're going away. They've given up,' whispered Ethne, who, caught in the kind of situation she was used to only before the TV cameras, had been staring at the gates as if hypnotized.

But the furniture van was not going away. It was backing across the road, the overhanging branches of the trees on the opposite bank whipping its top. The van lurched forward again – then back – then forwards. And then *sideways* – the van was slowly pulling sideways *across* the gates.

'They're trying to edge it right up against the gates,' said Julian, in low, urgent tones. 'I think they want to get up on to its roof, so that they can see over. We'll have to shut the door or they'll get a straight view into the stable. I'm going to wait here with Harry. Sylvia – you make the first move.'

There was another peal of thunder, this time from farther away. Nevertheless, Penny stirred restlessly behind them.

'No,' said Sylvia.

'Go on,' said Eve in panic. 'You're holding us all up, Sylvia. If we don't clear out quick, they'll be able to see us going – and they've got guns,' she finished on a little scream.

'No,' said Sylvia.

'Why not ?' squeaked Ethne.

'Because,' said Sylvia stolidly. Then she added, 'If Harry's going to stay with his horse, I'm going to stay with mine. Horrid brute'll be getting himself all upset next. Just like babies they are. Anyway, we can't all go 'n' leave Julian and Harry.'

Just then Julian swung the top of the half-door to. The whole stable was plunged in darkness. A frightened little gulp came from Ethne.

'It's all right, dear,' said Sylvia resignedly. 'We're all here – beastly horses and all.'

At that moment came an angry bellow :

'Who's there ? Come out of those stables!'

'That's King Mogg,' whispered Sandra shakily. 'He must have heard us.'

'He's on top of the van.' Julian had put his eye to the keyhole. 'There's another man scrambling up, too . . .'

And then, without warning, everything outside the gates went into confusion.

'Listen,' said Eve suddenly. 'There's another van coming –'

'There's cars coming –'

'Lots of cars –'

'What's happening?'

'Julian, what's happening?'

Up the hill, down the hill, converging with racing engines upon The Heron, it sounded to the children crouching behind the stable door as though a car rally were arriving at the gates. The cars drew up. Doors slammed. Shouting voices broke out up and down The Heron Ride. Suddenly the children peering through the crack of the door that Julian had cautiously opened, saw the top of the van sway violently as King Mogg and one of his friends jumped off. They heard heavy feet running up the road, more shouting, and the racing of more car engines.

And then – over all the noise – they heard the sound of – could it be *another* furniture van lumbering up the hill?

'It sounds like some sort of lorry,' said Sandra doubtfully.

As she spoke, they all jumped. For the darkness of the storm was all at once illuminated beyond the gates by a light so powerful that every leaf on every tree showed, and the square top of the furniture van turned to a dark block in an area as brilliantly lit as a theatre.

'Ooh,' squealed Ethne, dancing up and down with excitement. 'Ooh, it's the basher. It's the basher.'

'Who's bashing who?' said Sylvia apprehensively, as she craned for a better view behind Eve and Julian.

'No – no – it's the telly lights,' shrieked Ethne, twirling on her own axis with delight. 'From the camera. On that lorry. Ooh, they've really come. I knew they would –'

Just then a strange voice outside the gates shouted:

'Anybody there? Anybody in the stables?'

'Don't answer,' said Julian quickly. 'We don't know what's happening. We don't know who any of them are.'

'But if we don't answer, how will the telly boys know

I'm here?' Ethne tugged in alarm at Julian's elbow.

'*Anybody there? This is the police calling. Anybody there?*'

And then, above the uproar in the road – over the throbbing car-engines, the confused shouting, the clatter of the retreating thunder – rose one quiet, calm, authoritative voice that Sandra greeted with a private sob of relief:

'Now, dears, everything is quite all right. You can all come out now.'

'Miss Vaughan,' stated Sandra simply, to the stable at large.

Julian flung back the half-door, strode down the drive, battled with the heavy top and bottom bolts, and swung back the gates.

Caught in the dazzling light from the TV truck, the children advanced slowly down the drive – goggling and blinded. A tall police-officer had already engaged Julian in conversation. The furniture van was being gently manoeuvred to the side of the lane by a policeman. At angles across the road stood a number of black police cars, with policemen moving about them carrying walkie-talkie apparatus.

Sandra's eyes went directly to the opposite bank. There, under the trees, stood Miss Vaughan and a rather pale Adam – and, with his fingers threaded tightly into those of Miss Vaughan, Weary. With an expression of stunned horror, Weary was staring after a black police van which was moving slowly off down the hill.

'Well, dear,' said Miss Vaughan to Sandra. 'What a dreadful afternoon we have all had! And how very good you and Adam have been! Poor Weary –' and she looked compassionately down at the little boy – 'poor Weary is, I am afraid, very upset.'

'That wuz me grandfather. In that van,' croaked Weary

T—F

distractedly to Sandra. 'The police are taking him to prison.'

'Well, we don't know about prison,' said Miss Vaughan as comfortingly as she could. 'But –'

'The last we saw of King Mogg was up on top of that furniture van,' said Sandra, bewildered. 'He was shouting at us to come out. He couldn't even have known it was us –'

'Poor foolish Major Mogg,' said Miss Vaughan. 'I'm afraid he has got himself mixed up in a most unfortunate incident. It seems that there has been some very valuable horse stolen from one of the well-known studs near Newmarket. I read about it in *The Times* only this morning.'

'That wuz me grandfather – gone off in the black van . . .'

'We're going back to Long Meadow Cottage for tea soon, Weary,' said Miss Vaughan, bending down kindly over the distracted little boy.

'He *didn't* have a gun,' sobbed Weary. 'But I *did* see it.'

'I think,' said Miss Vaughan gently, 'that your grandfather only threatened to take his revolver with him. I think he was angry with your great-aunt, and he wanted to frighten her. Nobody – mercifully – seems to have been carrying guns.'

'Adam,' said Sandra, 'what did happen to you? Did you get your lift?'

But Adam was watching the furniture van. Something was happening. The men on the TV truck had trained the camera upon it, and two policemen were standing guard at the doors, while two more were letting down the ramp. The furniture van had become the focus of all attention. And – Sandra's mouth opened – there was Onkel Anton! Onkel Anton was being ushered up the ramp by a policeman, as if he were a visiting monarch. He disappeared inside the van.

'We got a lift right away into Ardsham,' said Adam, still watching the van. 'Nice chap who took us straight to the police station. And Miss Vaughan and Onkel Anton were still there. And we told them about King Mogg and the revolver. And everybody was very nice. And Miss Vaughan and a policeman went and fetched Queen Mogg from the decorators', which was practically next door. And she kicked up an awful show at the police station, and gave the whole thing away. And it turned out that she thought King Mogg had got himself mixed up in this business. She guessed, from something he'd let out, that he'd arranged to lend the stables of The Heron to the men who'd stolen the horse, to hide it for a couple of nights –'

'But *what* horse?' interrupted Sandra. 'Everybody's talking about a horse. *Where's* a horse?'

'*There*,' said Adam, pointing.

Sandra looked where Adam pointed. At first she could not believe her eyes. And then she drew a slow, quiet breath of long delight. There, walked down the ramp by Onkel Anton, moving supplely and with dignity, calmly unafraid of the lights and the people and the distant storm, came a grey horse. The last time that she had seen such a horse had been long ago, with Mother, when, with Mother's hand in hers, they had looked down together upon the arena of the Imperial Riding School in Vienna. And only once since had she been truly reminded of that afternoon –when she had gazed down upon Onkel Anton's faded photograph of such a horse, performing the *Levade* between the pillars in that same arena.

She stood, quietly watching. And, for a brief moment, everybody else – police, television men, everybody – fell silent as the beautiful animal came to a stop at the foot of the ramp, caught in the brilliant light, its aristocratic head raised, its widened nostrils sniffing the cool, sweet, rainy air of the woods.

Onkel Anton began to walk the horse up and down the lane. For everyone, except Sandra, the spell was broken. Television men and police stirred again. But Sandra slipped across the road to Onkel Anton.

'Is it a Lipizzaner?' she asked in an awed voice, ready now for any miracle that this strange afternoon could provide.

Onkel Anton smiled.

'No,' he said kindly. 'No, Sandra – not a Lipizzaner. Some day I will show you the Lipizzaners in Vienna. But you are seeing a very, very famous stallion. This is Silver Danger – and for Silver Danger great sums of money have been offered to his wise owner, and they have been refused. Now one rich and unscrupulous man abroad has too much wanted Silver Danger for his stud –'

'Miss Vaughan says it was in the papers,' put in Adam, who had just joined them, 'but only a tiny paragraph saying "Famous Stallion Kidnapped" –'

'By a gang that knew Major Mogg's friend – the friend with whom he stables his own horses, and so often visits,' nodded Onkel Anton. 'And so the little arrangement was made. The Heron stables – they are ready! Before the rest of the house, are the stables ready – and empty! The friend knows this. He tells his friends, "There is a place where Silver Danger can be hidden, until you can ship him to Europe." And so Major Mogg – he is approached. Who would suspect him – so famous an English rider!'

'No wonder he had had new bolts and a new padlock put on the gates,' said Sandra. 'And no wonder there were spare halters in his car, and a sack of feed in the stable –'

'It is sad,' said Onkel Anton. 'A man of such international reputation! But his sister, she say at the police station that he is short of money. The sale of the so-famous school – it did not go well. He has paid much money for Greens. The Heron costs more than he expects. And he is offered a great sum for his stables for two nights –'

'And he must have been bored with teaching little girls,' said Adam. 'I suppose he thought he could turn Greens into something –'

'And then found that he could not,' said Onkel Anton. 'It is a pity. He could have liked to make Eve and Sylvia and Julian happy. He could have enjoyed to teach Harry and Ethne. But no! He has mistaken what he can do –'

'What's going to happen to Silver Danger now?' asked Sandra, as she and Adam paced up and down the lane on the other side of Onkel Anton.

'There is a horse-box on its way out from Ardsham, with a groom from the Ardsham stables,' said Onkel Anton.

But Sandra's attention had been arrested elsewhere.

'What is happening?' she said.

'Oh,' said Adam, exasperated. 'It's Ethne. Julian told me a moment ago. He got it out of Sylvia –'

Framed between the Heron gate-posts, tip of tongue protruding between clenched teeth, Ethne was advancing on her pony to shouted instructions from the sound-man, who had posted himself by the gates.

'That's what she's been up to all along,' said Adam, with manly disgust. 'She rang her agent to say there was going to be a Teen-Age Strike, and wouldn't one of the TV companies be interested because she was going to be in it on a horse –'

'And they all fell for it!' said Sandra, awed by some people's silliness.

'They were short of material for their Children's programmes. And they sent along on the off-chance. And

just look at the scoop they've got! They've walked straight
in on the arrest of Silver Danger's kidnappers!'

Onkel Anton had led Silver Danger out of the range of
the blinding light from the basher. Adam drew nearer,
with mirthful countenance, to watch Ethne, like a ship
listing to port, sliding about the neck of her pony. Suddenly tired, Sandra retreated to the bank to find comfort
with Miss Vaughan.

But Miss Vaughan, with Weary, had disappeared.
Sandra guessed that a police car had taken them off to
Long Meadow Cottage. She looked up and down the lane.
The Greens contingent were in a huddle under a tree some
little way off. They were talking so busily that they had
not seen her. A policeman was standing over them, as if
he had been put in charge of Greens. She looked round for
Julian. But Julian was talking away to the men on the
TV truck. As she watched them, Adam left Ethne and
moved off to join Julian. Then Ethne finally slithered off
her pony, and pattered away to join Greens, while the
sound-man gingerly led her pony back to the stables of The
Heron.

Sandra spread her macintosh out on the bank, and sat
down upon it. The TV men had turned off the basher, so
that she found herself in the cool, grey light of the
departed storm, with the sun distantly straggling through
the clouds over the Downs. Only the sulky rumbling
beyond the horizon, and the dripping of the leaves, reminded her that there had been a storm.

Sitting quietly there by herself, she began to realize
that she was very tired. Every bone seemed to be aching.
It had been a long and, as Miss Vaughan had said, a dreadful afternoon. First of all, Weary's arrival through the
storm – and then seeing Adam go off to Ardsham without
her – and then the long ride up to The Heron on Toby –

and then the wait outside The Heron gates, with the storm beating down upon her and Toby – and then the frightening episode in the stables, with King Mogg and his anger only just beyond the gates. And now this ending – with police cars, and shouting, and the downfall of a famous rider, and Weary in distress. . . .

Just then there was another commotion among the police and the TV men. Sandra wearily turned her head. The horse-box for which everybody was waiting had hove into sight. As it slowly approached and drew up before the gates, she could see a plain-clothes man sitting in the front by the driver, and a young groom, bare-headed and eager-faced.

Sandra watched while the young groom got out, exchanged a few words with Onkel Anton, walked admiringly round Silver Danger, and then, with a horse-blanket over one arm, gently led him up into the fastness of the horse-box. The departure of Silver Danger was unspectacular. The police closed round the ramp. A moment later, smoothly, regally, the horse-box began to move off down the hill. Silver Danger had begun his homeward journey.

As Silver Danger went out of her life, Sandra leaned forward from the bank, watching until the horse-box had rounded the bend. When he had gone, she realized that to the tiredness of her bones was now added a stealing depression, a slow aching of the heart. Silver Danger was the nearest she had seen to those horses she and Mother had loved together. She began to feel that never again would she see a horse like him. For her there would never be anything but horses like Toby.

And then she went on, down, down the long ladder of despair. She began to reflect that only if she were lucky would there be a Toby! She remembered that she would

be staying only a little while longer at Long Meadow. Then
the shadow of Uncle Arthur began to lengthen towards
her, the hated house in Bayswater to start up, like a fort-
ress, before her eyes. Soon Long Meadow, Miss Vaughan,
and Onkel Anton would themselves become shadows –
memories like the Lipizzaners, and the Beautiful Cities,
and the houses they had lived in, and the people who had
loved her and Adam, and whom she and Adam had loved
so much. Sandra sat back on the bank, fighting her old
arch-enemy, the little gulp, which was once again threatening to rise up her throat and besiege her with tears.

But this time, she was too quick for the little gulp. She
fought it back, because the recollection of Toby reminded
her that he was still stabled up in The Heron. There was
Toby to be ridden home!

She stumbled to her feet. In spite of the sun, which was
beginning to break through into the lane, she felt cold
with dreariness and fatigue. Adam and Julian were still
poking round the TV truck. Round the gates of The Heron
the police were sorting themselves out. Dimly she realized
that, further down the lane, some crisis had arisen in the
Greens group. Sylvia was openly in tears. Harry was gesti-
culating. Nobody saw her pass. Exhaustedly, she made
her way between the policemen at the gates. As if cannon-
balls weighted her tired feet, she walked up the drive of
The Heron.

XV

INSIDE the stable it was cool and dim and peaceful. The
sunlight was beginning to steal through the slatted windows, motes of dust idling in its long shafts. Only a barely
perceptible movement down the line of stalls betrayed
that – for the first time perhaps in a quarter of a century –
the stables were occupied.

Sandra took no notice of the Greens horses. She walked
noiselessly to the stall on the extreme left of the doorway.
Toby was still placidly standing, staring straight ahead

at the blank, white-washed wall. Seen in silhouette, he looked stocky, ordinary, and his nose pure Roman.

She went straight into Toby's stall, and buried her face in his damp, dishevelled mane. 'You were splendid!' she whispered down his ear. 'The way you came clopetty-clop up to those gates!'

At the farther end of the stable she heard a footfall. She raised her head. In the half-light she could discern Onkel Anton, a bridle over one arm, quietly coming down the stable towards her.

'You have come to take Toby home – yes?' he said. 'But, Sandra, there is no need. I am asked by the police to escort back the children to Greens –'

'But there isn't a horse for you,' said Sandra.

'It will arrange itself,' said Onkel Anton, 'if Ethne, who is I think, now frightened of her horse, rides Toby. Then I, who am light, will ride Ethne's pony. And you – who are tired – and Adam and Julian, who also has no horse, will return to Long Meadow in a police car.'

It was a relief to have no more riding that day! Sandra looked directly at Onkel Anton across Toby.

'Did you mean it just now?' she said. 'Did you mean it when you told me that some day you would show me the Lipizzaners in Vienna?'

At that moment, she felt that if the invitation had been only Onkel Anton's joke, she would die with silent misery.

Onkel Anton regarded her keenly.

'But yes,' he said. 'I mean it.'

'Because,' said Sandra, desperately, 'I could start to save the fare straight away. I'd rather come to Vienna some day than go to the White City next year – if Uncle Arthur will ever let me.'

Onkel Anton was silent for a moment. Then he said gently, 'Miss Vaughan – she has told me about Uncle

Arthur, and the cousins, and the noisy house in London. Sandra – these bad, bad things, they do not last for ever. It is only for a while, Sandra –'

'That's what Adam says,' whispered Sandra, staring out over Toby's tail at the sunlight reaching across the doorway. 'But when you're in it, it seems for ever and for ever –'

'Nobody expects that you should like it,' answered Onkel Anton. 'Why should you? You have not much in common with your Uncle Arthur, I think. Why should one like to be with people with whom one does not share? Why should one think that one will fit there? And already look what you have done – you have begun to make your own way out –'

'It's easy at Long Meadow,' said Sandra. 'And it's not only me that matters. It's Adam, too. He doesn't want to go back to Uncle Arthur, either.'

'But for both of you there are the good things to come,' said Onkel Anton firmly. 'For you and for Adam. And – yes – there will be the Lipizzaners in the future. Not always, Sandra, does one spend one's life riding a Toby!'

'Toby's so good,' said Sandra loyally.

But Onkel Anton was feeling in his pocket. He took out his wallet, and began to fumble through its contents, as she had seen him on his first evening at Long Meadow. He found what he wanted, held it critically for a moment to the light. Then he passed it to Sandra.

'Certainly – certainly together we will see the Lipizzaners in Vienna,' declared Onkel Anton. 'And I give you a token to keep to remind you that we do. And when I meet your train at the big station in Vienna, you shall lean out of the window, and wave it, and cry, "Here I am. Although I am taller than when you saw me at Long Meadow, I am still Sandra –" '

'Oh,' said Sandra, in sudden rapture, 'but it's the photograph of the horse performing the *Levade*. It's you when you were a young man. Oh, I'd love to have it. Oh, I'll drawing-pin it up by Weary's little picture of him doing the Highland fling –'

'He has, for the moment, fallen on his nose, that one,' murmured Onkel Anton.

But Sandra had raised her head anxiously from the photograph. 'I'd forgotten,' she said. 'It's all you've got to remind you that you were once a groom in the Imperial Riding School. You can't part with it. I mustn't have it –'

Onkel Anton was laughing at her. 'Oh-ho,' he said, 'I am not so unselfish. There are at Andelsbach other photographs. He performs, that horse, many of the great movements. But that is the best. I give you the best. And you shall always ask for the best, Sandra – even if, for the moment, the answer is a Toby – and an Uncle Arthur!'

He accompanied Sandra to the doorway before he returned to his saddling of the Greens' horses. Sandra passed through the door, and out into the sunlit drive, carrying her token. She went down the drive, and out into The Heron Ride, as if she had suddenly been made a princess. . . .

The moment that she appeared in the lane, they began to stream towards her. Adam and Julian followed slowly. But Sylvia, with Ethne, Eve and Harry, came charging down the lane.

'*They're not going to let us stay at Greens!*'

Hoarse with horror, Harry had hurtled past Sylvia upon Sandra. 'That policeman says so. He's been left in charge of us. He says we're going to ride the horses back to Greens –'

'With your Austrian gentleman who's been helping with that creature they kidnapped,' sobbed Sylvia. 'And then – oh, Sandra – we're to be taken straight to the police station –'

'Because there isn't anybody at Greens to look after us. Did you ever hear anything like it?' demanded Harry. 'The magistrates are going to say we're in need of care and protection –'

'And they're going to get in touch with our people to come and fetch us. Mum and Dad won't be back for ages. Oh, I don't want to go to Gran,' wept Sylvia. 'She's cross, and she's *old* –'

'But what about Miss Mogg?' said Sandra. 'She's not under arrest. They'll let her come back to Greens. She can look after you all for the rest of the time, can't she?'

'Oh, tell her, somebody,' implored Sylvia. 'You haven't heard what's happened. We've been telling Adam –'

'It's that policeman told them,' said Adam. 'Queen Mogg can't go back to Greens. Apparently after we left the police station, she went on having hysterics. And she kept saying nothing would get her back to Greens. And they've sent her off by ambulance to some hospital –'

'There you are. She's come unstuck. Oh, *nobody* wants us. We *can't* go to the police station –'

'And it won't *do* for me to be seen at a *police station*,' wailed Ethne.

'Julian, what about you?' said Sandra.

But Julian did not answer Sandra. He was watching the only member of the Greens contingent who had not yet spoken.

'Eve?' said Julian questioningly.

Eve was standing remotely at the back of the group. She was gazing out through the trees, as if she could see far beyond the hidden Mill Pool. Only one long, dirty stain down her face showed that she had shed so much as a tear. Her handkerchief was clenched into a ball in her

right hand. As Julian addressed her, she slowly thrust
it down into her jodhpur pocket, and withdrew her gaze
levelly to meet his.

'Eve?' said Julian again.

'I'm not going to leave Greens,' said Eve.

There was that in Eve's voice that caused a silence to
fall upon the whole group.

'I'm not going to have Ma sent for,' said Eve. 'She
wouldn't come, even if I told 'em where she was. She's
with friends on the Riviera. Bobby's there, too. Bobby's
the chap she's going to marry. And I don't know where
Dad is, and I don't care. I hate him. I hate Ma. I hate
Bobby. The lot – I hate them. I'm going to stay at Greens
by myself.'

With a swaggering turn of her pretty little dark head,
Eve turned back to her contemplation of distance.

Everybody stared, horrified. Then:

'Oh, whatever are we all going to do?' said Sylvia slowly.
There was no answer.

At that moment Onkel Anton came briskly out of the
Heron gates, spoke a word to the police, and came across
the road. Sandra saw him look from one tear-stained face to
the next. But Onkel Anton made no comment other than
to say, 'We are ready – yes? Then together we will take the
horses –'

He was interrupted by a small gasp of panic from
Ethne, whose face had suddenly become suffused with
pink:

'*I don't want to ride back. I don't want to go on a horse
again. I nearly fell off again just now –*'

'You will not fall off if I come with you, I think,' said
Onkel Anton coaxingly. 'And see – you will ride the kind
Toby.'

Unmoved by Ethne's public loss of nerve, Onkel Anton

began, like a kind shepherd, to marshal his little party towards The Heron. Sandra, Julian and Adam watched from the bank.

The riding party went in total silence. Only the droop of their shoulders as they trudged round the gate-posts spoke of the disaster that had befallen the beloved Greens. Sandra realized that nobody had told Onkel Anton. Since Eve's manifesto, what was to happen had seemed too bad to be spoken aloud. Nevertheless, Sandra had the impression that Onkel Anton had divined the despair that had invaded all hearts.

Also in total silence, Sandra and the two boys sat down on the macintosh which was still spread out upon the bank. At last Adam said in an undertone to Julian, as though both were attending a funeral, 'Your people'll come and drive you home?'

'Yes,' said Julian shortly.

They sat for some time longer, saying nothing. Sandra thought that Onkel Anton was taking some time to mount his riders. The police by the gate had begun to fidget and peer up the drive. At length one policeman detached himself, and came across the road.

'Sorry to keep you hanging about,' he said. 'But my orders is to see them all off the premises before I drive you home.'

'What on earth are they doing?' said Adam.

He got to his feet, and walked over to the Heron gates. Sandra and Julian watched him go and return in dejected silence.

'Nothing's happening at all,' he reported in disgust. 'They're all standing around Onkel Anton outside the stables. He's talking to them – that's all!'

'It's a bit late to be giving Greens a riding lesson,' observed Julian gloomily.

They relapsed again into silence. The policeman consulted his watch. 'I've got to drive them all from Greens to the police station after I drop you,' he said.

The three said nothing. There was still nothing to say.

'I suppose we'll spend the night in a rest-centre,' said Julian at length.

The policeman rejoined his friends at the gate. With the passing of the storm, the lane was once again becoming close and airless. The midges had come joyfully out in force. Sandra tugged at the bracken-stalk for a fan. She waved it lethargically to and fro.

But at last, she let it rest. She clasped her knees and put her head down upon them. The drama of King Mogg was over. The comedy of Ethne and the TV camera was over. Onkel Anton had given her his token, and the Lipizzaners were in the future. But Eve was not in the future. Eve was in the present.

Sitting on the bank, waiting for the emergence of Greens, Sandra's mind kept returning to Eve – to Eve, standing in the lane, savagely locked within her own loneliness. Sandra felt that before this afternoon, she had scarcely looked at Eve, had never thought to single her plight out from the others. Now, suddenly, here was Eve reminding her of that other kind of refugee that Adam had remembered. Adam's kind of refugee on that distant wintry day outside the Stefanskirche had been fierce and tough and angry ... Oh, but Eve – for all her coldness – was not tough ... Sandra gave a small, unheard, inner cry for Eve. Because of what it had been like for her during those four bad, black years with Uncle Arthur, she knew just a little of what it was like to be Eve. It was terrible to be Eve. ...

Deeply, deeply in her thoughts, Sandra started to angle for an idea, for some solution for Greens. She fished in her mind as patiently as Adam in the Long Meadow stream.

But ideas do not always come just for the bidding. . . .

After a few moments, the refugees outside the Stefanskirche reminded her of something else. She raised her head.
Adam was sitting hunched, his arms also round his knees,
his gaze glumly fastened upon the Heron gates.

'Did anything happen about Paul at the police station?'
she asked.

'He's found,' said Adam absently. 'The police rang London, while Eulalia and Onkel Anton were there. He'd
walked into a police station near the Strand a couple of
hours before, and told them he'd lost the name *and* the
address.'

'When's he coming?'

'Tomorrow afternoon.'

'Why not today?'

'Because,' said Adam with an air of much patience,
'because he wants to go and see St. Andrew's-by-the-Ward-
robe.'

'What on earth – it's a *church* –'

'Oh, it's all *right*,' said Adam crossly. 'Eulalia *quite*
understands. He's known about it all his life. He's always
wanted to see it. It's like you with those Lipizzaners –'

'Oh.'

'I shall probably,' announced Adam with detachment,
'show him my brass-rubbings.'

Just then there was a stirring by the Heron gates. The
policemen were looking expectantly up the drive as if
royalty were due. The trio on the bank sat upright.

The slow clip-clop of the horses could be heard coming
down the drive. Round the gate and out into The Heron
Ride came the little cavalcade. Harry led on Penny. Sylvia
followed. After Sylvia came Eve. On a leading-rein swiftly
fashioned from rope, Ethne brought up the rear, with
Onkel Anton.

As Greens passed, the policemen came to something very like attention.

'Something's happened to them!' said Sandra slowly, as she stared after the riders.

'Not to their riding.' But Adam was frowning, as if puzzled.

Then Julian said thoughtfully: 'It wasn't a riding lesson that Onkel Anton was giving them!'

Nobody – thought Sandra – would ever know what Onkel Anton had said to Greens up by the stables of The Heron. Nobody would ever ask. Nobody would probably tell. But in those long minutes it seemed that somehow Onkel Anton had returned to Greens its courage. One and all they smiled at Sandra, Julian and Adam as they passed down The Heron Ride. Those who had wept still wore their tear-stains. But nobody's shoulders sagged with hopelessness, and everybody's head was high. Greens rode with courage.

Onkel Anton was riding Ethne's horse. Sandra watched him as the horses rounded the first bend on the downward curve of the hill. It was the first time they had seen Onkel Anton mounted. Riding in King Mogg's place, he seemed to belong to the little contingent in a way that had never been King Mogg's. He rode serenely, vigilantly, and with authority. Oh, thought Sandra, it should have been Onkel Anton. . . .

Sandra remained leaning forward, as if she had got stuck.

'Come on,' said Adam, who had leapt to his feet, as if Greens had communicated its spirit to him.

Sandra remained, fingering the photograph in her pocket, apparently in a trance.

'Come *on*,' said Adam impatiently. 'The police are shutting the gates, and that one's waiting to drive us home.'

'Adam,' said Sandrā. 'Have you got that money in your pocket that you didn't telephone Miss Vaughan with at the station?'

'Yes,' said Adam, jingling it.

'Then give it to me. Ask that policeman to wait three minutes.'

'For goodness' sake, Sandra —'

Sandra began to run. She ran round the first corkscrew. She could see Greens disappearing round the second. She ran on and on. The tiredness seemed to be creeping through her whole body. She could see the roofs of the cottages belonging to the hamlet above the Mill Pool. In another minute she would see the telephone kiosk.

The sound of the horses' hooves died away among the trees. She stumbled into the telephone kiosk. Oh, but it was stiflingly hot inside. She managed to keep the door open with her heel. Supposing Miss Vaughan had not gone straight back to Long Meadow! Everything, now, hinged on Miss Vaughan.

She took the money from her pocket. She dialled the Long Meadow number, and waited. Her brain seemed to be spinning round and round with heat and tiredness. But a small smile of excitement curved her lips.

And then she pushed the money into the slot.

'Miss Vaughan!' she whispered, and louder because Miss Vaughan down at Long Meadow had calmly told her to speak up, 'Oh, Miss Vaughan, I've had an idea! Can't you tell the magistrates about Onkel Anton? Can't Onkel Anton go to Greens for the next three weeks, and look after them all, and teach them to ride?'

The little smile of excitement had crept into her voice with the delight and the simplicity of her idea. It was so simple an idea Sandra wondered nobody else had thought of it.

'Onkel Anton knows all about people being refugees! He'd stop them all from being quite such refugees! Oh, Miss Vaughan, they'd be properly taught at last by a groom of the Imperial Riding School. And you could tell the magistrates that none of them – Eve – none of them, would ever be *quite* such refugees ever again!'

Epilogue

EARLY the next morning, Sandra was kneeling on the window-seat in her room. The cottage was still wrapped in sleep. But she could hear Adam just beginning to move quietly about his bedroom. Before he could settle to cleaning his fishing-tackle, Sandra leaned over and gave three muted taps on the wall. Three muted taps came in reply, signifying that cleaning would be deferred, and Adam along in a minute.

Sandra put her head out of the window. The air was a little sharper than usual. But the day was going to be hot, though not so torrid as before the storm. This morning she noticed for the first time that there was something about the sunlight that reminded her of autumn.

'What do you think it would be like in the garden of The Heron in the autumn?' she said in an undertone, as Adam tiptoed into the room.

'*Bonfires!*' said Adam. 'All those leaves!'

'Raggy chrysanthemums, smelling like bonfires. Those purple Michaelmas daisies, with little thin spider's webs across them –'

'All down the sides of those grass alleys. We shan't be here then,' said Adam.

'We're here now,' said Sandra wisely. 'Let's go down to the stream.'

The grass beyond the white gate was grey with the dew. The children walked carefully barefoot down the meadow.

'The soles of my feet are getting brown and hard,' said

183

Sandra proudly. 'When I first came I couldn't have walked barefoot.'

There were spirals of mist smoking upon the surface of the stream. The water looked black and forbidding, like that other early morning when they had gone through the woods to the Mill Pool, and had spotted King Mogg's demesne, high and golden in the sunlight.

As they clambered down the bank to inspect the new level of the stream, Adam said, 'Eulalia was saying last night that she thought King Mogg would be allowed out on bail. He wasn't really involved with the kidnapping of Silver Danger. Someone'll have to guarantee that he turns up to answer the charge, but she's sure he won't be kept in prison till the trial.'

'The magistrate would never let him come back and be in charge at Greens,' said Sandra.

'But he doesn't want to come back,' said Adam sombrely. 'Eulalia said that he'd seen his solicitor at the police station. King Mogg was sick as mud over the whole thing –'

'Poor man!'

'Now, *Sandra*! And he was thankful to hand over to Onkel Anton. So everybody's pleased.'

'Miss Vaughan did move quickly,' said Sandra contentedly, savouring once again her hour of triumph. 'She'd got on to the police about Onkel Anton before he'd got Greens down The Heron Ride. When she went round and told Greens, she said Sylvia hugged her, and Harry was speechless –'

'First time in his life,' grunted Adam, bending down to gaze into the dark water.

'She said that Eve never said anything. She just strolled over to the window, and looked out. Miss Vaughan said she thought Eve would like to have cried with relief. . . .'

But Adam had stopped listening. 'I thought I saw a fish,' he said.

'Can you see anything in that water but the reflection of the sky?'

'I believe the fish have come back after the storm. I don't believe there ever was an otter.'

'Julian said he didn't think it was an otter,' said Sandra.

'I wonder if we could build a raft for this stream. Now there's more water, we could float down to the Mill Pool. I wonder if Paul would be interested in building a raft –'

'Julian would,' said Sandra.

'Julian's not going to be free for raft-building,' said Adam. 'Onkel Anton'll work them pretty hard.'

'He'll work them hard, but they'll love it,' prophesied Sandra. 'They'll have *fun* again.'

Hanging on to a dipping branch, they bent down to send two twigs towards the Mill Pool on the faster-moving current.

'Onkel Anton's a fine teacher,' observed Adam, as his twig foundered against a floating bough. 'He'd got Ethne off that leading-rein by the time they reached Greens.'

'What a shock it must have given Toby – suddenly finding himself tied to a leading-rein!' said Sandra.

'Probably pooped up his morale no end,' said Adam. 'Probably never thought of himself as A Dangerous Pony before!'

They turned their backs on the stream. They began to drift slowly back towards the cottage, the sun already warm on their necks and arms.

'Onkel Anton told me he wants to keep Ethne on Toby for the moment,' said Sandra. 'He'd like to teach her as he's taught me – from the beginning.'

'Well, that makes sense,' said Adam. Then he stopped dead in the middle of the meadow, and looked at Sandra.

'But what are you going to ride if Onkel Anton borrows Toby for Ethne?'

'I suppose – nothing very much – for the moment,' said Sandra. 'But I didn't quite like to say. The Vicar's lending him to Greens in the mornings. He says he's going to invest in a motor mower. Anyway, Toby can't be ridden all that much. He's not really a riding pony, and he's too fat –'

'He must have lost *pounds* yesterday—'

'So there we are!' said Sandra.

'But – dash it!' Adam began to splutter with indignation. 'You want to ride! Why should you be the one to be left out?' Then suddenly he forgot his wrath, and stiffened like a pointer. 'Look –' he said in mollified tones, 'Eulalia's putting out the breakfast cups. Oh, how very hungry I am!'

The latch of the white gate into the cottage garden was already warm to the touch. The sunlight was lying along its bars, patching the grass, the tops of the cypresses, and the windfalls lying in the grass under the apple trees. Apart from the windfalls, and a few bowed mallows and snapdragons, the storm had left Long Meadow as peaceful as it had found it. Sandra slid herself along the bench at the trestle table, suddenly thankful that everybody's storms had – for a little while – passed. Even the prospect of no Toby failed to disturb her peace. She clasped her hands round her cup of coffee, and looked happily down Long Meadow, beyond the beech trees and up to the Downs, where the shadows from the clouds were lazily passing.

'I thought,' said Miss Vaughan from the top of the table, 'that we would have an early breakfast while Weary was still asleep.'

Adam cracked the top of his egg. 'I do so agree,' he said politely. Then he added, 'If we're really going to keep him here until his mother's ready for him, do you suppose that he's going to wake us all up *every* night, having nightmares?'

'No,' returned Miss Vaughan calmly, 'I think Weary will soon be happy again. He will enjoy being here with Sandra, and his troubles will be forgotten.'

'Oh, *look!*' said Sandra.

Chin tucked down into his favourite spot in the hedge, cheeks wreathed with bryony and bramble, Toby stood watching them from the Glebe. Everybody began to laugh.

'He looks like Bottom after Titania has finished garlanding him,' said Adam. Then he remembered. He turned anxiously to Miss Vaughan.

'There's nothing for Sandra to ride now,' he said accusingly.

'It doesn't matter,' said Sandra equably. She might feel less equable later in the day. But just now – with the sun and the hot coffee, and the return of the peaceful days – nothing much mattered. Beyond Toby's ears, she could see the cows slowly stringing across the Glebe. There they went, the boy with the stick idling behind them. Sandra's eye followed the leader meandering daintily towards the gate.

Then she realized that Miss Vaughan was speaking to her.

'I thought Onkel Anton had told you last night,' Miss Vaughan was saying, 'but I suppose we were all so busy, arranging the affairs of Greens –'

'Told me what?' said Sandra, puzzled.

'Told her what?' echoed Adam.

'That he had had a talk with the police about his taking over at Greens. Onkel Anton is an alien.'

'But what's that got to do with it?' said Adam. 'They *can't* think Onkel Anton is a spy.'

'Running a riding school in the absence of the owner is really a professional job,' Miss Vaughan said. 'The police were wondering if Onkel Anton would want payment. It's difficult paying aliens who are here without labour permits. There are all sorts of regulations.'

'I wouldn't have thought Onkel Anton was the kind of man who'd ever think about being paid,' said Adam.

'Onkel Anton was very clever,' said Miss Vaughan. 'He didn't want to be paid. He made a little speech to the police telling them so. But he said that it would give him great pleasure if one of his hosts – who had been the first to give him such a warm welcome – were allowed to ride with Greens. He would like, he said, to be permitted to teach her with the others.'

For a moment neither child said anything. Very slowly this news then began to sink in.

'Do you mean –' began Adam.

'That I'm to – oh, you can't mean it – that I'm to ride one of Greens' horses ?' said Sandra slowly.

Miss Vaughan smiled and nodded. 'Onkel Anton's expecting you to take Toby round to Greens after breakfast. Major Mogg knows all about it. He's glad for Onkel Anton to ride his horse, and for you to ride Ethne's pony.'

Sandra rose to her feet. The soaring happiness was too much to be borne sitting. 'Oh,' she said with quiet rapture, 'oh, that was my wish – in the station booking-hall. I wanted us all to learn to ride, and here we are all going to –'

'Didn't I tell you your luck had . . . turned ?' said Adam.

'It's like a fairy-tale,' said Sandra.

'You deserve your luck,' said Miss Vaughan. 'People in fairytales go through quite a bit, and work quite hard, to get their luck.'

'And what about my luck?' demanded Adam, nudging his Eulalia.

'Well,' said Miss Vaughan consideringly. 'You've fished that stream hard enough. I expect the fish are there waiting for you after the storm. But in the meantime – I can see that Sandra is dying to saddle Toby – do you want to fish this morning? Or what would you enjoy doing?'

'What would you enjoy doing?' said Adam, with equal courtesy.

'I must ice Paul's cake first.'

'If you could put Onkel Anton's name upon it, we might bring you back Paul,' said Adam gravely.

'But after that, I am at your disposal.'

'I'd like us to go up to The Heron,' said Adam, looking up beyond the stream to where the big, grey house stood, sunlit among the shadowy trees. 'Seeing that one day I'm going to buy The Heron, I'd like us to potter round the garden, and look at the lead heron, and walk along the terrace. And we can talk about what will happen to The Heron *now* –'

'The Heron's future, now, nobody knows,' said Miss Vaughan. 'And strictly speaking, we shall both be trespassing. But I don't think anybody will mind. I'm only afraid the police may have locked the gates.'

'Not to worry,' said Adam graciously. 'I will show you a way in that you'll simply love. Surprise! Surprise!'

'Well,' said Sandra, moving away under the apple trees towards the Glebe. 'Well, I'll be back at lunch time. Perhaps we could go down to the stream after lunch, and fish. And then there'll be Paul –'

'And then, after tea,' said Adam, 'there'll be you!'

'Me?'

Sandra paused, the shadows from the leaves passing across her face.

'You'll be up *there*!' said Adam, waving his hand up
beyond the beech trees, beyond the woods, to the line of
Downs. 'You've forgotten! We can watch you from the
garden this evening. We can stand down by the white
fence, watching you cantering along up there with the
sun in your face. And we'll be saying to each other,
"There's old Sandra, looking just as if she's riding a Lipizzaner." '

also by Mary Treadgold

RETURN TO THE HERON

Who was going to buy The Heron, the beautiful
old house with its stables and garden? What
would a new guardian be like for Sandra and
Adam? What could Adam do about his gift for
drawing? 'All *I* want is just a *horse*,' said Sandra
in a moment of wild longing: but how could that
be?

This is Mary Treadgold's second book about
Sandra and Adam, about The Heron and riding.

These are other Knights

More books about horses and riding

Primrose Cumming
Four rode home

Monica Edwards
Rennie goes riding

Ruby Ferguson
Jill's Gymkhana
A stable for Jill
Jill has two ponies
Jill enjoys her ponies
Jill and the perfect pony
Jill's riding club
Jill's pony trek
Pony jobs for Jill
Rosettes for Jill

Ask your local bookseller, or at your public library for details of other Knights, or write to the Editor-in-Chief, Knight Books, Arlen House, Salisbury Road, Leicester LE1 7QS